"It Only Took Us Five Minutes To Get Married—No Reason Why The Divorce Should Take Any Longer."

"Glad you see it that way." He gave a sharp nod, and his hand went to the inside pocket of his suit. "Of course, I'll want to cover any inconvenience." He extracted a gold pen and a brown leather checkbook, flipping open the cover and glancing at her. "A million?"

Kaitlin blinked in confusion. "A million what?"

He breathed a sigh of obvious impatience. "Dollars," he stated. "Don't play coy, Kaitlin. You and I both know this is going to cost me."

Was he that desperate?

Wait a minute. *Was* he desperate?

Dear Reader,

I have a passion for historic buildings—big or small, opulent or plain. From the passageways of the Tower of London to the faded boards of a broken-down shed on a lonely prairie highway, I love to imagine who built a house, who walked its halls, who lived, who loved and who might have died there all those years ago.

Billionaire Zach Harper is descended from pirates. His family castle, built on an island off the coast of New York, is a living museum and the centerpiece of his heritage. But when he accidentally marries architect Kaitlin Saville at a wild Vegas office party, everything is at risk.

I hope you enjoy Zach and Kaitlin's story. I modeled the Harper family castle after the real-life Craigdarroch Castle in Victoria, British Columbia. If you're interested, there's a link to the castle on my website.

Happy reading!

Barbara

www.barbaradunlop.com

BARBARA DUNLOP

THE CEO'S ACCIDENTAL BRIDE

Published by Silhouette Books
America's Publisher of Contemporary Romance

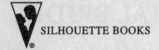

SILHOUETTE BOOKS

Recycling programs for this product may not exist in your area.

ISBN-13: 978-0-373-73075-9

THE CEO'S ACCIDENTAL BRIDE

This edition published by arrangement with Harlequin Books S.A.

For questions and comments about the quality of this book please contact us at Customer_eCare@Harlequin.ca.

® and TM are trademarks of Harlequin Books S.A., used under license. Trademarks indicated with ® are registered in the United States Patent and Trademark Office, the Canadian Trade Marks Office and in other countries.

Visit Silhouette Books at www.eHarlequin.com

Printed in U.S.A.

Books by Barbara Dunlop

Silhouette Desire

Thunderbolt over Texas #1704
Marriage Terms #1741
The Billionaire's Bidding #1793
The Billionaire Who Bought Christmas #1836
Beauty and the Billionaire #1853
Marriage, Manhattan Style #1897
Transformed Into the Frenchman's Mistress #1929
*Seduction and the CEO #1996
*In Bed with the Wrangler #2003
*His Convenient Virgin Bride #2009
The CEO's Accidental Bride #2062

*Montana Millionaires: The Ryders

BARBARA DUNLOP

writes romantic stories while curled up in a log cabin in Canada's far north, where bears outnumber people and it snows six months of the year. Fortunately she has a brawny husband and two teenage children to haul firewood and clear the driveway while she sips cocoa and muses about her upcoming chapters. Barbara loves to hear from readers. You can contact her through her website at www.barbaradunlop.com.

For my fabulous editor, Kathryn Lye

One

Zach Harper was the last person Kaitlin Saville expected to see standing in the hallway outside her apartment door. The tall, dark-haired, steel-eyed man was the reason she was packing her belongings, the reason she was giving up her rent-controlled apartment, the person who was forcing her to leave New York City.

Facing him, she folded her arms across her dusty blue Mets T-shirt, hoping her red eyes had faded from her earlier crying jag and that no tear streaks remained on her cheeks.

"We have a problem," Zach stated, his voice crisp, and his expression detached. His left hand was clasped around a black leather briefcase.

He wore a Grant Hicks suit and a pressed, white shirt. His red tie was made of fine silk, and his cuff links were solid gold. As usual, his hair was freshly cut, face freshly shaved, and his shoes were polished to within an inch of their lives.

"*We* don't have anything," she told him, curling her toes into the cushy socks that covered her feet below the frayed hem of her faded jeans.

She was casual, not frumpy, she told herself. A woman had a right to be casual in her own home. Where Zach Harper had no right to be in her home at all. She started to close the door on him. But his hand shot out to brace it.

His hand was broad and tanned, with a strong wrist and tapered fingers. No rings, but a platinum Cartier watch with a diamond face. "I'm not joking, Kaitlin."

"And I'm not laughing." She couldn't give one whit about any problem the high-and-mighty Zach Harper might encounter during his charmed life. The man not only got her fired, but he also had her blackballed from every architectural firm in New York City.

He glanced past her shoulder. "Can I come in?"

She pretended to think about it for a moment. "No."

He might be master of his domain at Harper Transportation and at every major business function in Manhattan, but he did not have the right to see her messy place, especially the collection of lacy lingerie sitting under the window.

He clenched his jaw.

She set her own, standing her ground.

"It's personal," he persisted, hand shifting on the briefcase handle.

"We're not friends," she pointed out.

They were, in fact, enemies. Because that was what happened when one person ruined another person's life. It didn't matter that the first person was attractive, successful, intelligent and one heck of a good dancer. He'd lost all rights to...well, anything.

Zach squared his shoulders, then glanced both ways down the narrow corridor of the fifty-year-old building. The light was dim, the patterned carpets worn. Ten doors opened into this particular section of the fifth floor. Kaitlin's apartment was at the end, next to a steel exit door and a fire alarm protected by a glass cover.

"Fine," he told her. "We'll do it out here."

Oh, no, they wouldn't. They wouldn't do anything anywhere, ever again. She started to step back into the safety of her apartment.

"You remember that night in Vegas?" he asked.

His question stopped her cold.

She would never forget the Harper corporate party at the Bellagio three months ago. Along with the singers, dancers, jugglers and acrobats who had entertained the five-hundred-strong crowd of Harper Transportation's high-end clients, there was a flamboyant Elvis impersonator who'd coaxed her and Zach from the dance floor to participate in a mock wedding.

At the time, it had seemed funny, in keeping with the lighthearted mood of the party. Of course, her sense of humor had been aided that night by several cranberry martinis. In hindsight, the event simply felt humiliating.

"The paper we signed?" Zach continued in the face of her silence.

"I don't know what you're talking about," she lied to him.

In fact, she'd come across their mock wedding license just this morning. It was tucked into the lone, slim photo album that lived in her bottom dresser drawer beneath several pairs of blue jeans.

It was stupid to have kept the souvenir. But the glow from her evening on Zach's arm had taken a few days to fade away. And at the time she'd put the marriage license away, those happy minutes on the dance floor had seemed somehow magical.

It was a ridiculous fantasy.

The man had destroyed her life the very next week.

Now, he drew a bracing breath. "It's valid."

She frowned at him. "Valid for what?"

"Marriage."

Kaitlin didn't respond. Was Zach actually suggesting they'd signed a real marriage license?

"Is this a joke?" she asked.

"Am I laughing?"

He wasn't. But then he rarely laughed. He rarely joked, either. That night, she'd later learned, was quite the anomaly for him.

A cold feeling invaded her stomach.

"We're married, Kaitlin," he told her, steel eyes unflinching.

They were not married. It had been a lark. They'd been playacting up there on the stage.

"Elvis was licensed by the state of Nevada," said Zach.

"We were drunk," Kaitlin countered, refusing to believe such a preposterous claim.

"He filed a certificate."

"How do you know that?" Her brain was revving into overdrive, calculating the possibilities and the potential consequences.

"Because my lawyers tell me so." He gave a meaningful glance past her shoulder, into the apartment. "Can I please come in?"

She thought about her mystery novels covering the couch, the entertainment magazines that were sitting out on the coffee table, the credit card and bank statements in piles beside them, revealing her shopping habits for the past month. She remembered the telltale, half-eaten package of Sugar Bob's doughnuts sitting out on the counter. And, of course, there was the box of sexy underwear on full display in the afternoon sunshine.

But, if he was telling the truth, it wasn't something she could ignore.

She gritted her teeth and ordered herself to forget about his opinion. Who cared if he found out she had a weakness for Sugar Bob's? In a matter of days, he'd be out of her life. She'd leave everything she'd ever known, start all over in another city, maybe Chicago or Los Angeles.

Her throat involuntarily tightened at the thought, and her tears threatened to freshen.

Kaitlin hated being uprooted. She'd started over so many times already, leaving security and normalcy behind as she moved from one childhood foster home to another. She'd been in this small apartment since she started college. And it was the only place that had ever felt remotely like home.

"Kaitlin?" he prompted.

She swallowed to clear the thick emotions from her throat. "Sure," she told him with grim determination, stepping aside. "Come on in."

As she shut the door, Zach took in the disarray of packing boxes littering the apartment. There wasn't anywhere for him to sit down, and she didn't offer to clear a chair. He wouldn't be staying very long.

Though she tried to ignore it, her glance shifted involuntarily to the underwear box. Zach tracked her gaze, his resting on the mauve-and-white silk teddy her friend Lindsay had bought her for Christmas last year.

"Do you mind?" she snapped, marching over to pull the cardboard flaps shut.

"Not at all," he muttered, and she thought she heard a trace of amusement in his tone.

He was laughing at her. Perfect.

The cardboard flaps sprang back open again, and she felt the unwelcome heat of a blush. She turned to face him, placing her body between Zach and her underwear.

Behind him, she spied the open box of Sugar Bob's. Three of the doughnuts were missing, transferred from the white cardboard and cellophane container to her hips around nine this morning.

Zach didn't appear to have an ounce of fat on his well-toned body. She'd be willing to bet his breakfast had consisted of fruit, whole grains and lean protein. It was probably whipped up by his personal chef, ingredients imported from France, or maybe Australia.

He perched his briefcase on top of a stack of DVDs on her end table and snapped open the latches. "I've had my lawyers draw up our divorce papers."

"We need lawyers?" Kaitlin was still struggling to comprehend the idea of marriage.

To Zach.

Her brain wanted to go a hundred different directions with that inconceivable fact, but she firmly reined it in. He might be gorgeous, wealthy and intelligent, but he was also cold, calculating and dangerous. A woman would have to be crazy to marry him.

He swung open the lid of the briefcase. "In this instance, lawyers are a necessary evil."

Kaitlin reflexively bristled at the stereotype. Her best friend, Lindsay, wasn't the least bit evil.

For a second, she let herself imagine Lindsay's reaction to this news. Lindsay would be shocked, obviously. Would she be worried? Angry? Would she laugh?

The whole situation was pretty absurd.

Kaitlin anchored her loose auburn hair behind her ears, reflexively tugging one beaded jade earring as a nervous humor bubbled up inside her. She cocked her head and waited until she had Zach's attention. "I guess what happens in Vegas sometimes follows you home."

A muscle twitched in his cheek, and it definitely wasn't from amusement. She felt a perverse sense of satisfaction at having put him even slightly off balance.

"It would help if you took this seriously," he told her.

"We were married by Elvis." She clamped determinedly down on a spurt of nervous laughter.

Zach's gray eyes flashed.

"Come on, Zach," she cajoled. "You have to admit—"

He retrieved a manila envelope. "Just sign the papers, Kaitlin."

But she wasn't ready to give up the joke. "I guess this means no honeymoon?"

He stopped breathing for a beat, and there was something familiar about the way his gaze flicked to her lips.

She was struck by a sudden, vivid memory, instantly sobering her.

Had they kissed that night in Vegas?

Every once in a while, she had a fleeting image of his mouth on hers, the heat, the taste, the pressure of his full lips. She imagined that she could remember his arms around her waist, pulling her tight against his hard body, the two of them molding together as if they belonged.

In the past, she'd always chalked it up to a fevered dream, but now she wondered...

"Zach, did we—"

He cleared his throat. "Let's try to stay on track."

"Right." She nodded, determinedly pushing the hazy image out of her mind. If she'd kissed him even once, it was the worst mistake of her life. She detested him now, and the sooner he disappeared, the better.

She reached out her hand and accepted the envelope. "It only took us five minutes to get married, no reason why the divorce should take any longer."

"Glad you see it that way." He gave a sharp nod, and his hand went to the inside pocket of his suit. "Of course, I'll want to cover any inconvenience." He extracted a gold pen and a brown leather checkbook, flipped open the cover and glanced at her. "A million?"

Kaitlin blinked in confusion. "A million what?"

He breathed a sigh of obvious impatience. "Dollars," he stated. "Don't play coy, Kaitlin. You and I both know this is going to cost me."

Her jaw involuntarily dropped a notch.

Was he crazy?

He waited expectantly.

Was he desperate?

Wait a minute. *Was* he desperate?

She gave her brain a little shake. She and Zach were husband and wife. At least in the eyes of the law. Clearly, she was a problem for him. She doubted the high-and-mighty Zach Harper ran into too many problems. At least, none that he couldn't solve with that checkbook.

Huh.

Interesting.

This time, Kaitlin did chuckle, and tapped the stiff envelope against the tabletop. She certainly didn't want Zach's money, but she sure wouldn't say no to a little payback. What woman would?

This divorce didn't have to happen in the next five minutes. She'd be in New York for at least another couple of weeks. For once in his life, Mr. Harper could bloody well wait on someone else's convenience.

She took a breath, focused her thoughts and tried to channel

Lindsay. Lindsay was brilliant, and she'd know exactly what to do in this circumstance.

Then, the answer came to Kaitlin. She raised her brows in mock innocence. "Isn't New York a joint property state?"

Zach looked confused, but then his eyes hardened to flints.

He was angry. Too bad.

"I don't recall signing a prenup," she added for good measure.

"You want more money," he spoke in a flat tone.

All she really wanted was her career back.

"You got me fired," she pointed out, feeling the need to voice the rationale for her obstinacy.

"All I did was cancel a contract," he corrected.

"You had to know I'd be the scapegoat. Who in New York City is going to hire me now?"

His voice went staccato. "I did not like your renovation design."

"I was trying to bring your building out of the 1930s." The Harper Transportation building had infinite potential, but nobody had done anything to it for at least five decades.

He glared at her a moment longer. "Fine. Have it your way. I got you fired. I apologize. Now how much?"

He wasn't the least bit sorry for having her fired. He didn't care a single thing about her. The only reason he'd even remembered her name was because of the accidental marriage. And he'd probably had to look that up.

She squared her shoulders beneath the dusty T-shirt, determined to take this victory. "Give me one good reason why I should make your life easier?"

"Because you don't want to be married any more than I do."

He had a fair point there. The mere thought of being Zach Harper's wife sent a distinct shiver coursing its way up her spine.

It was distaste. At least she was pretty sure the feeling was distaste. With any other man, she might mistake it for arousal.

"Mrs. Zach Harper." She pretended to ponder, warming to

her stubborn stance as she purposely slowed to note her half-packed apartment. "Don't you have a roomy penthouse on Fifth Avenue?"

He clicked the end of his pen, slowly lowering it to his side. "Are you daring me to call your bluff?"

She cracked her first genuine smile in three months. He wouldn't do it. Not in a million years. "Yeah," she taunted boldly. "Go ahead. Call my buff."

He stepped closer, and an annoying buzz of awareness tickled its way through her stomach. They stared each other down.

"Or you could leave the divorce papers," she offered with mock sweetness. "I'll have my lawyer read them over next week."

"Two million," he offered.

"Next week," she retorted, trying not to show her shock at the exorbitant figure. "Summon up some patience, Zachary."

"You don't know what you're doing, *Katie*."

"I'm protecting my own interests," she told him.

And there was something to be said for that. Seriously. Who could guess what his lawyers had hidden in the divorce documents?

They were both silent. Horns honked and trucks rumbled by five floors below.

"I don't trust you, Zach," she informed him tartly. Which was completely true.

His expression hardening by the second, he stuffed the pen into his pocket, then deliberately tucked the checkbook away. He closed and latched the briefcase, and sharply straightened the sleeves of his jacket.

Seconds later, the door slammed shut behind him.

Zach slid into the passenger seat of the black Porsche Carrera idling at the curb outside Kaitlin's Yorkville apartment building and yanked the door shut behind him.

"Did she sign?" asked Dylan Gilby, as he slipped the gearshift into First.

Zach tugged the seat belt over his shoulder and clicked the latch into place. "Nope."

He normally prided himself on his negotiating skills. But there was something about Kaitlin that put him off his rhythm, and the meeting had been a colossal failure.

He didn't remember her being so stubborn. To be fair, he hadn't known her particularly well. They'd met a few times before the party, but it was only in passing while she was working on the renovation plans for his office building. He remembered her as smart, diligent, fun-loving and beautiful.

He had to admit, the beautiful part certainly still held true. Dressed to the nines in Vegas, she was the most stunning woman in a very big ballroom. Even today, in a faded baseball T-shirt and jeans, she was off the charts. No wonder he'd gone along with Elvis and said "I do." He was pretty sure, in that moment, he did.

"You offered her the money?" asked Dylan.

"Of course I offered her money." Zach had wanted to be fair. Well, and he'd also wanted the problem solved quickly and quietly. Money could usually be counted on to accomplish that.

"No go?" asked Dylan.

"She's calling her lawyer," Zach admitted with a grimace, cursing under his breath. Somehow, he'd played it all wrong. He'd blown his chance to end this neatly, and he had nobody to blame but himself.

Dylan flipped on his signal light and checked the rearview mirror on the busy street. He zipped into a tight space between a Mercedes and an old Toyota. "So, basically, you're screwed."

"Thank you for that insightful analysis," Zach growled at his friend. Harper Transportation could well be on the line here, and Dylan was cracking jokes?

"What are friends for?" joked Dylan.

"Procuring single malt." If ever there was a time that called for a bracing drink, this was it.

"I have to fly today," said Dylan. "And I get the feeling you'll need every brain cell functioning."

Zach braced his elbow against the armrest as the car angled its way through traffic on the rain-dampened street. He reviewed the conversation with Kaitlin like a postgame tape. Where had he messed it up?

"Maybe I should have offered her more," he ventured, thinking out loud. "Five million? Do people say no to five million?"

"You might have to tell her the truth," Dylan offered.

"Are you out of your mind?"

"Clinically, no."

"Tell her that she's inherited my grandmother's entire estate?"

Hand the woman control on a silver platter? Did Dylan want to guarantee Zach was ruined?

"She did, in fact, inherit your grandmother's estate," Dylan pointed out.

Zach felt his blood pressure rise. He was living a nightmare, and Dylan of all people should appreciate the outrageousness of the situation.

"I don't care what kind of paperwork was filed by the Electric Chapel of Love," Zach growled. "Kaitlin Saville is not my wife. She is not entitled to half of Harper Transportation, and I will die before—"

"Her lawyer may well disagree with you."

"If her lawyer has half a brain, he'll tell her to take the two million and run." At least Zach hoped that was what her lawyer would say.

The two of them were married. Yes. He'd have to own that particular mistake. But it couldn't possibly be a situation his grandmother had remotely contemplated when she wrote her will. There was the letter of the law, and then there was the spirit of the law. His grandmother had never intended for a stranger to inherit her estate.

He had no idea if New York was, in fact, a joint property state. But even if it was, he and Kaitlin had never lived together. They'd never had sex. They'd never even realized they were married. The very thought that she'd get half of his corporation was preposterous.

"Did you think about getting an annulment?" asked Dylan.

Zach nodded. He'd talked to his lawyers about that, but they weren't encouraging. "We never slept together," he told Dylan. "But she could lie and say that we did."

"Would she lie?"

"What do I know? I thought she'd take the two million." Zach glanced around, orienting himself as they approached an entrance to Central Park. "We going anywhere near McDougal's?"

"I'm not getting you drunk at three in the afternoon." Dylan shook his head in disgust as he took a quick left. The Porsche gripped the pavement, and they barely beat an oncoming taxi.

"Are you my nursemaid?" asked Zach.

"You need a plan, not a drink."

In Zach's opinion, that was definitely debatable.

They slowed to a stop for a red light at another intersection. Two taxi drivers honked and exchanged hand gestures, while a throng of people swelled out from the sidewalk in the light drizzle and made their way between the stopped cars.

"She thinks I got her fired," Zach admitted.

"Did you?"

"No."

Dylan sent him a skeptical look. "Is she delusional? Or did you do something that resembled getting her fired?"

"Fine." Zach shifted his feet on the floor of the Porsche. "I canceled the Hutton Quinn contract to renovate the office building. The plans weren't even close to what I wanted."

"And they fired her," Dylan confirmed with a nod of comprehension.

Zach held up his palms in defense. "Their staffing choices are none of my business."

Kaitlin's renovation plans had been flamboyant and exotic in a zany, postmodern way. They weren't at all in keeping with the Harper corporate image.

Harper Transportation had been a fixture in New York City for a hundred years. People depended on them for solid reliability and consistency. Their clients were serious, hardworking people who got the job done through boom times and down times.

"Then why do you feel guilty?" asked Dylan as they swung into an underground parking lot off Saint Street.

"I don't feel guilty." It was business. Nothing more and nothing less. Zach knew guilt had no part in the equation.

It was not as if he should have accepted inferior work because he'd once danced with Kaitlin, held her in his arms, kissed her mouth and wondered for a split second if he'd actually gone to heaven. Decisions that were based on a man's sex drive were the quickest road to financial ruin.

Dylan scoffed an exclamation of disbelief as he came parallel with the valet's kiosk. He shut off the car and set the parking break.

"What?" Zach demanded.

Dylan pointed at Zach. "I know that expression. I stole wine with you from my dad's cellar when we were fifteen, and I remember the day you felt up Rosalyn Myers."

The attendant opened the driver's door, and Dylan dropped the keys into the man's waiting palm.

Zach exited the car, as well. "I didn't steal anything from Kaitlin Saville, and I certainly never—" He clamped his jaw shut as he rounded the polished, low-slung hood of the Porsche. The very last element he needed to introduce into this conversation was Kaitlin Saville's breasts.

"Maybe that's your problem," said Dylan.

Zach coughed out an inarticulate exclamation.

"You married her," Dylan said, taking obvious satisfaction in pointing that fact out as they crossed the crowded parking lot. "You must have liked her. You said yourself you haven't slept with her. Maybe you're not so much angry as horny."

"I'm angry. Trust me. I can tell the difference." Zach's interest in Kaitlin was in getting rid of her. Anything else was completely out of the question.

"Angry at her or at yourself?"

"At *her*," said Zach. "I'm just the guy trying to fix the problem here. If she'd sign the damn papers, or if my grandmother hadn't—"

"It's not nice to be mad at your grandmother," Dylan admonished.

Zach wasn't exactly angry with Grandma Sadie. But he was definitely puzzled by her behavior. Why on earth would she put the family fortune at risk? "What was she *thinking?*"

Dylan stepped up onto the painted yellow curb. "That she wanted your poor wife to have some kind of power balance."

An unsettling thought entered Zach's brain. "Did my grandmother talk to you about her will?"

"No. But she was logical and intelligent."

Zach didn't disagree with that statement. Sadie Harper had been a very intelligent, organized and capable woman. Which only made her decision more puzzling.

After Zach's parents were killed in a boating accident when he was twenty, she'd been his only living relative. They'd grown very close the past fourteen years. She was ninety-one when she died, and had grown increasingly frail over the past year. She'd passed away only a month ago.

Zach thought he was ready.

He definitely wasn't.

He and Dylan headed into the elevator, and Dylan inserted his key card for the helipad on top of the forty-story building.

"She probably wanted to sweeten the deal," Dylan offered, with a grin. He leaned back against the rail, bracing his hands on either side as the doors slid shut. "With that kind of money on the table, you'll have a fighting chance at getting a decent woman to marry you."

"Your faith in me is inspiring."

"I'm just sayin'…"

"That I'm a loser?"

The elevator accelerated upward.

Dylan happily elaborated. "That there are certain things about your personality that might put women off."

"Such as?"

"You're grumpy, stubborn and demanding. You want to drink scotch in the middle of the day, and your ass isn't what it used to be."

"My ass is none of your business." Zach might be approaching thirty-five, but he worked out four times a week, and he could still do ten miles in under an hour.

"What about you?" he challenged.

"What about me?" Dylan asked.

"We're the same age, so your ass is in as much danger as mine. But I don't see you in a hurry to settle into a relationship."

"I'm a pilot." Dylan grinned again. "Pilots are sexy. We can be old and gray, and we'll still get the girls."

"Hey, I'm a multimillionaire," Zach defended.

"Who isn't?"

The elevator came smoothly to a halt, and the doors slid open to the small glass foyer of the helipad. One of Dylan's distinctive yellow-and-black Astral Air choppers sat waiting on the rooftop. A pilot by training, Dylan had built Astral Air from a niche division of his family's corporation to one of the biggest flight service companies in America.

Dylan gave a mock salute to a uniformed technician as he and Zach jogged to the chopper and climbed inside.

He checked a row of switches and plugged in the headset. "You want me to drop you at the office?"

"What are your plans?" asked Zach. He wasn't in a hurry to be alone with his own frustrations. He had a lot of thinking to do, but first he wanted to sleep on it, start fresh, maybe forget that he'd screwed up so badly with Kaitlin.

"I'm going up to the island," said Dylan. "Aunt Ginny's been asking about me, and I promised I'd drop in."

"Mind if I tag along?"

Dylan shot him a look of surprise. Aunt Ginny could most charitably be described as eccentric. Her memory was fading, and for some reason she'd decided Zach was a reprobate. She also liked to torture the family's Stradivarius violin and read her own poetry aloud.

"She has two new Pekingese," Dylan warned.

Zach didn't care. The island had always been a retreat for him. He needed to clear his head and then come up with a contingency plan.

"I hope your dad still stocks the thirty-year-old Glenlivet," he told Dylan.

"I think we can count on that." Dylan started the engine, and the chopper's rotor blades whined to life.

Two

A week later, Kaitlin met her best friend, law professor Lindsay Rubin, in the park behind Seamount College in midtown. The cherry trees were in full bloom, scenting the air, their petals drifting to the walkway as the two women headed toward the lily pad–covered duck pond. It was lunchtime on a Wednesday, and the benches were filled with students from the college, along with businesspeople from the surrounding streets. Moms and preschool kids picnicked on blankets that dotted the lush grass.

"I finished reviewing your papers," Lindsay said, swiping her shoulder-length blond hair over the shoulders of her classic navy blazer while they strolled their way down the concrete path.

Kaitlin and Lindsay's friendship went back to their freshman year at college. Social Services had finally stepped out of Kaitlin's life, and Lindsay had left her family in Chicago. On the same floor of the college dorms, they'd formed an instant bond.

They'd stayed close friends ever since, so Lindsay knew that Zach had ruined Kaitlin's career, and she applauded Kaitlin's desire for payback.

"Am I safe to sign?" asked Kaitlin. The sunshine was warm against her bare legs and twinkled brightly where it reflected off the rippling pond. "And how soon do I have to let him off the hook?"

Lindsay grinned in obvious delight. She pressed the manila envelope against Kaitlin's chest, and Kaitlin automatically snagged it.

"Oh, it's better than that," she said.

"Better than what?" Kaitlin was puzzled

Lindsay chuckled deep in her chest. "I mean, you can name your own ticket."

"My ticket to what?"

Why was Lindsay talking in riddles?

"Life," Lindsay elaborated in a singsong voice. "What do you want? A mansion? A jet? A billion dollars?"

"I told you, I said no to the money." Kaitlin hadn't changed her mind about the money. She didn't want what she hadn't earned. "And what do you mean a billion? He was talking about two million."

"It's more than just two million." Lindsay shook her head in what appeared to be amazement. "It's Sadie Harper herself."

Kaitlin lifted her hands, palms up, to signal her incomprehension. She assumed Sadie Harper must have something to do with Zach Harper, but that was as far as she got with the connection. What did the woman have to do with his money?

Lindsay lowered her voice, sounding decidedly conspiratorial as she moved closer to Kaitlin, her gaze darting dramatically around them. "Sadie was the matriarch of the Harper family. She died a month ago at the Harper house on Serenity Island."

The pathway split, and Lindsay eased Kaitlin toward the route that skirted the pond. Their high heels clicked against the smooth, sun-warmed concrete.

Kaitlin still didn't understand Lindsay's point.

"I read a copy of her will," said Lindsay. "You, my girl, are in it."

"How can I be in it?" This conversation was making less sense by the minute. Kaitlin didn't know Sadie Harper. Up until this minute, she'd never even heard of Sadie Harper.

"In fact," Lindsay continued, a lilt of delight in her voice, "*you* are the sole beneficiary."

Kaitlin instantly halted, turning to peer at Lindsay with narrowed eyes. Traffic zipped past on Liberty, engines roaring, horns honking. Cyclist and pedestrian traffic parted around them, some people shooting annoyed looks their way.

Lindsay tugged on Kaitlin's arm, moving them off to the side of the pathway. "She left her entire estate to Mrs. Zachary Harper."

"Get out," Kaitlin breathed.

"I am dead serious."

Kaitlin stepped farther aside to make room for a pair of cyclists skirting the edge of the path. "How did she even know about me?"

"She didn't." Lindsay gave her head a shake. "That's the beauty of it. Well, part of the beauty of it. The whole thing is truly very beautiful."

"Lindsay," Kaitlin prompted with impatience.

"The will holds her estate in trust until Zach gets married," said Lindsay. "But he's already married so, in the eyes of the law, you own fifty percent of Harper Transportation."

Kaitlin's knees went weak.

No wonder Zach had seemed desperate.

No wonder he was in such a hurry to get rid of her.

"So, what do you want?" Lindsay asked again, a giggle at the end of the question.

Speechless, Kaitlin shoved the envelope back at Lindsay, overwhelmed by the thought of what was at stake. She took a step away and shook her head in silent refusal.

"I don't want anything," she finally managed to reply.

"Don't be ridiculous," Lindsay cajoled.

"The wedding was a joke," Kaitlin reminded her. "It was a mistake. I didn't mean to marry him. And I sure don't deserve half his company."

"Then take the money instead," Lindsay offered reasonably.

As if that made it better. "I'm not taking his money, either."

Lindsay held up her palms in exasperation. "So, what do you want? What's the payback?"

Kaitlin thought about it for a moment. "I want him to sweat."

Lindsay chuckled and linked her arm with Kaitlin's, turning her to resume their walk. "Trust me, honey." She patted her on the shoulder. "He is definitely sweating."

"And I want a job," said Kaitlin with conviction. That was what she'd lost in this debacle. She needed her career back.

"I don't want free money," she told Lindsay, voice strengthening. "I want a chance to prove myself. I'm a good…no, I'm a *great* architect. And all I want is a fair shot at proving it."

The path met up with the sidewalk, and Lindsay tipped her head and stared up at the Harper Transportation sign on the pillar-adorned, ten-story concrete building across the street. "So, ask him for one," she suggested.

Kaitlin squinted at the massive blue lettering. She glanced to Lindsay, then again at the sign. Suddenly, the possibilities of the situation bloomed in her brain.

A slow smile grew on her face. "There's a reason I love you," she said to Lindsay, giving her arm a squeeze. "*That* is a brilliant plan."

And it was exactly what she'd do. She would make Zach Harper give her a job. She'd make him give her the job that should have been hers in the first place—developing designs for the renovation of his corporate headquarters.

She'd pick up right where she'd left off. In fact, she'd come up with an even better concept. Then, once she'd proven to him and to the world that she was a talented architect, she'd sign whatever papers he needed her to sign. He'd have his company back, and she'd have her life back. And, most importantly, she wouldn't have to leave New York City.

The light turned green, and she tugged on Lindsay's arm. "You're coming with me."

Lindsay hesitated, staying on the curb. "I have a class now."

"We'll be quick," Kaitlin promised.

"But—"

"Come on. I need you to spout some legalese to scare him."

"Trust me, he's already scared." But Lindsay started across the street.

"Then it'll be easy," Kaitlin assured her, stepping up on the opposite curb then mounting the short concrete staircase.

They made their way across the small serviceable lobby of the Harper Transportation building. Kaitlin had been in the building many times, so she knew Zach's office was on the top floor.

While they took the groaning elevator ride up twenty stories, she straightened her short black skirt and adjusted her sleeveless, jade-green sweater, anchoring the strap of her small handbag. She moistened her lips as they exited the elevator. Then she determinedly paced down the narrow hallway to Zach's receptionist.

"I'm here to see Zach Harper," Kaitlin announced with as much confidence as she could muster.

Her pulse had increased, and her palms were starting to dampen. She was suddenly afraid the plan wouldn't work. Like a drowning woman who'd been tossed a life vest, she was afraid her chance would float away before she could grab on to it.

"Do you have an appointment?" the young brunette woman asked politely, glancing from Kaitlin to Lindsay and back again. Kaitlin had seen the woman from a distance while working on the project for Hutton Quinn, but they'd never been introduced.

"No," Kaitlin admitted, realizing the odds were slim that Zach was available at that particular moment.

Lindsay stepped forward, standing two inches taller than Kaitlin, her voice telegraphing professionalism and importance. "Tell him it's a legal matter," she said to the receptionist. "Kaitlin Saville."

The woman's head came up, curiosity flaring briefly in her blue eyes. "Of course. One moment, please." She rose from her wheeled desk chair.

"Thanks," Kaitlin whispered to Lindsay, as the receptionist walked down the hallway that stretched behind her desk. "I knew you'd come in handy."

"I'll send you a bill," Lindsay responded in an undertone.

"No, you won't." Kaitlin knew her friend better than that. Lindsay had never charged her for anything in her life.

"Ten minutes from now, you'll be able to afford me," Lindsay joked.

"Send Zach the bill," Kaitlin suggested, a nervous sense of excitement forming in her belly. If this worked. If it actually worked...

"Will do," Lindsay promised.

The receptionist returned, a practiced, professional smile on her face. "Right this way, please."

She led them past a few closed doors to the end of the hallway where a set of double doors stood open on a big, bright, burgundy-carpeted room.

She gestured them inside, and Kaitlin entered first.

If she thought Zach had looked impressive standing in her apartment last week, it was nothing compared to what his office did for him. The fine surroundings reeked of power, and he was obviously in his element.

His big desk was walnut with inset cherry panels. A matching credenza and hutch were accented with cherry wood drawers, and a bookcase opposite showcased leather-bound volumes and nautical carvings. The desk chair was also leather, and high-backed with carved wood arms. Two guest chairs flanked the front of his desk, while a meeting table stood in an arched window alcove.

As Kaitlin crossed the thick carpet, Zach came to his feet. As usual, he wore a perfectly pressed, incredibly well-cut suit. His usual white shirt was crisp and bright. The necktie was gold this time, with a subtle silver thread that picked up the sunlight.

"Thank you, Amy." He nodded to the receptionist, who closed the doors as she left the room.

His gaze flicked to Lindsay and he quirked a questioning brow in her direction.

"My lawyer," Kaitlin explained to him. "Lindsay Rubin."

"Please sit down." Zach gestured to the leather guest chairs.

But Kaitlin chose to remain standing. "I'll sign your papers," she told him.

Zach's glance went back to Lindsay, then returned to Kaitlin. The barest hint of a smile twitched his full lips, and there was a definite flare of relief in his gray eyes.

"But I want two things," Kaitlin continued.

Though she knew she ought to enjoy this, she was far too nervous to get any pleasure out of watching him sweat.

This had to work.

It simply *had* to.

Zach's brow furrowed, and she could almost feel him calculating dollar figures inside his head.

"One—" she counted on her fingers, struggling to keep a quaver from forming in her voice "—our marriage stays secret." If people found out she was married to Zach, the professional credential of renovating his building would mean less than nothing. The entire city would chalk it up to their personal relationship.

"Two," she continued, "you give me a job. Renovation design director, or some similar title."

His eyes narrowed. "You want a job?"

"Yes," she confirmed.

He appeared genuinely puzzled. "Why?"

"I'll need an office and some support staff while I finish planning the renovations to your building. Since you already have those things available here…"

He was silent for a full three seconds. "I'm offering you money, not a job."

"I don't want your money."

"Kaitlin—"

She squared her shoulders. "This is not negotiable, Zach. I get free rein, carte blanche. I do your renovation, my way, and—"

He leaned forward, tenting his fingers on the polished desktop. "Not a hope in hell."

"Excuse me?"

They glared at each other for a drawn-out second while a thousand emotions skittered along her nervous system.

He was intimidating. He was also undeniably arousing. He was both her problem and her solution. And she was terrified this chance would somehow slip through her fingers.

Then Lindsay spoke up, her voice haughty and authoritarian as she stepped into the conversation. "You should know, Mr. Harper, that I've provided Ms. Saville with a copy of Sadie Harper's will, as filed with the probate court."

The room went to dead silent.

Nobody moved, and nobody breathed.

Kaitlin forced herself to straighten to her full height. She crossed her arms over her chest, letting his stunned expression boost her confidence.

"I'll divorce you, Zach," she told him. "I'll sign the entire company over to you. Just as soon as I have my career back."

His furious gaze settled on Kaitlin. His tone turned incredulous. "You're *blackmailing* me?"

Sweat prickled her hairline, anxiety peaking within her. "I'm making you a deal."

Several beats ticked by in thick silence, while her stomach churned with anxiety.

His expression barely changed. But finally, he gave a single, curt nod.

Her heart clunked deep in her chest, while a wave of relief washed coolly over her skin.

She'd done it.

She'd bought herself a second chance.

She doubted Zach would ever forgive her. But she couldn't let herself care about that. All that mattered was she was back on the job.

From beneath the stained concrete porch of the Harper Transportation building, Kaitlin stared at the rain pounding down on Liberty Street. It was the end of her first full day of work, and her nerves had given way to a cautious optimism.

Zach hadn't made her feel particularly welcome, but she did have a desk, a cubbyhole of a windowless office, with a drafting table and a bent filing cabinet. And, though other staff members seemed confused by the sudden change in the renovation project, one of the administrative assistants had introduced her around and offered to help out.

Kaitlin inhaled the moist May air. Fat raindrops were splashing on the concrete steps, forming puddles and rivulets on the pavement below. She glanced at the gray sky and gauged the distance to the subway staircase in the next block. She wished she'd checked the weather report this morning and tossed an umbrella into her bag.

"I trust you found everything you need?" Zach's deep voice held a mocking edge behind her.

Kaitlin twisted, taking in his towering height and strong profile against the backdrop of his historic building. She was forced to remind herself that she was in the driver's seat in this circumstance. She should make him nervous, not the other way around.

"Could you have found me a smaller office?" she asked, attempting to go on the offensive. He was obviously making some kind of a point by relegating her to a closet. It didn't take a genius to figure out he was attempting to put her in her place.

"Haven't you heard?" His mouth flexed in a cool half smile, confirming her suspicions. "We're renovating."

"I notice *your* office is plenty roomy," she persisted, hoping to give him at least a twinge of guilt.

"That's because I own the company." His expression hinted that he also owned a decent portion of the world.

She arched a meaningful brow in his direction, feeling a little more in control when his expression wavered. "So do I," she pointed out.

Her victory was short-lived.

"You want me to evict a vice president for you?" Left unsaid was the understanding that while he could easily give her special treatment, they both knew it would raise questions amongst the staff, potentially compromising her desire to keep their personal relationship a secret.

"You have nothing between the executive floor and a closet?" Of course, the last thing she wanted to do was call attention to herself. He had to treat her no better and no worse than any other employee. Right now, it certainly appeared he was treating her worse.

"Take your pick," Zach offered with a careless shrug. "I'll kick someone out."

Kaitlin hiked up her shoulder bag. "And they'll know it's me."

"You do own the company," he drawled.

She rolled her eyes. "Just treat me like you would anyone else."

"That seems unlikely." He nodded to a shiny, black late-model town car cruising up to the curb. "Can I give you a lift?"

She slid him an incredulous glance. He had to be kidding.

"Hop into the boss's car after my first day of work?" Right. That would work well to keep her under the radar.

"You afraid people will get the wrong idea?"

"I'm afraid they'll get the right idea."

His mouth quirked again. "I have some papers you need to sign."

The rain wasn't letting up, but she took a tentative step forward, muttering under her breath. "No divorce yet, Mr. Harper."

He stepped into the rain beside her, keeping pace, his voice going low as hers. "They're not divorce papers, Mrs. Harper."

The title on his lips gave her a jolt. She'd spent the day trying to forget about their circumstances and focus on getting started at her job. But she was beginning to realize forgetting their circumstances was going to be nearly impossible.

They were married, *married*.

She tipped her head, surreptitiously taking in his profile, the dark eyes, the furrowed brow and the small scar on his right cheekbone. She tried to imagine an intimate relationship, where they joked and touched and—

"Kaitlin?"

She gave herself a firm mental shake, telling herself to get control. "What kind of papers?"

He glanced around, obviously confirming a sufficient buffer of space between them and the other Harper employees heading out the doors. "Confirmation of my positions as the president and CEO."

"What are you now?"

"President and CEO." His gunmetal eyes were as dark and impenetrable as the storm clouds. He was not a man who easily gave away his emotions. "There's been a change in the company ownership," he explained.

It took a moment for the enormity of his words to sink in. Without her signature, his position in the company was in jeopardy. He couldn't do what he'd always done, and he couldn't be who he'd always been, without her consent on paper.

Something hard and cold slid though her stomach.

It wasn't right that she had this kind of power. All she wanted was to do her job. She didn't want to have to sift through her confusing feelings for Zach. And she sure didn't want to have to analyze the circumstances and decide if they were fair.

They weren't. But then neither was the alternative.

"Get in the car, Kaitlin," he told her. "We need to get this signed and settled."

She couldn't help but note the stream of employees exiting from the building. Even as they dashed down the rainy steps, most of them glanced curiously at Zach. Climbing into his car in full view of a dozen coworkers was out of the question.

She leaned slightly closer, muffling her voice. "Pick me up on Grove, past the bus stop."

He gave a subtle but unmistakable eye roll. "You don't think that's a bit cloak-and-dagger?"

"I'm trying to blend," she reminded him. Her plan to rescue her career would come to a screeching halt if people had any inkling that she had some leverage over Zach.

"You'll get soaked," he warned her.

A little water was the least of her worries.

Well, except for what it would do to her shoes. They'd been on sale, her only pair of Strantas. She loved what they did for her legs, and they looked great with anything black.

She braced herself, mentally plotting a path around the worst of the scattered puddles.

"Have a nice evening, Mr. Harper," she called loud enough for passersby to hear as she trotted down the stairs.

She made her way along the sidewalk, surging with the crowd toward the traffic light at the corner. When it turned green, she paced across the street, avoiding numerous black umbrellas in her path and hopping over the gurgle of water flowing against the opposite curb.

On the other side, she negotiated her way to the edge of the sidewalk, raking her wet hair back from her forehead and tucking it behind her ears. She swiped a few raindrops from her nose then extracted her cell phone, pressing the speed dial as she hustled toward the bus stop shelter.

"Kaitlin?" came Lindsay's breathless voice.

"What are you doing?"

"Riding the bike."

Kaitlin pictured Lindsay on the stationary bike crammed into the small living space of her loft. "I'm going to be late for dinner."

"What's going on?" Lindsay huffed.

As she wove her way through the wet crowd, Kaitlin lowered her voice to mock doom. "I'm about to get into a big black car with Zach Harper."

"Better send me the license plate number."

Kaitlin cracked a grin, comforted by Lindsay's familiar sense of humor. The two women had known each other so long, they were almost always on the same wavelength. "I'll text it to you."

A deep, classic-rock bass resonated in the background. A fixture whenever Lindsay exercised. "Why are you getting in his car?"

"He wants me to sign something."

"Better let me read it first."

"I will if it looks complicated," Kaitlin promised. "He says it's to reconfirm him as president and CEO." Not that she trusted everything Zach said. In fact, thus far, she trusted exactly nothing of what Zach said.

"It could be a trick," Lindsay warned.

Kaitlin grinned into the phone. "There is yet another reason I love you."

"I've got your back. Seriously, Katie, if you see the words *irreconcilable* or *absolute* I want you to run the other way."

"Will do." Kaitlin caught sight of the black car. "Oops. There he is. Gotta go."

"Call me when you're done. I want details. And dinner." There was a gasp in Lindsay's voice. "I definitely still want dinner."

"I'll call," Kaitlin agreed, folding her phone and tucking it into the pocket of her purse as Zach swung open the back door of his car and hopped out onto the sidewalk next to her.

He flipped up the collar of his gray overcoat and gestured her inside. She gathered her own wet coat around her and ducked to climb in.

"Lunatic," he muttered under his breath.

"Lucky for you we're not having children," she said over her shoulder as she settled into the seat.

"Lucky for me we're not buying plants." He firmly shut the door behind her before walking around the vehicle to get in behind the driver.

She shook the rainwater from her fingertips, smoothing her soaked jacket and frowning at her soggy bag. "Green and Stafford in Yorkville," she said to the driver, getting an unwelcome glimpse of herself in the side mirror.

"The penthouse, Henry," Zach corrected.

"You're not dropping me off?" She wasn't sure why his bad manners surprised her. Zach was all about his own convenience. His minions obviously didn't factor in on his radar.

"Henry will take you home later," he said.

Later? She raised her brow in a question.

"The papers are at my penthouse."

Of course they were. Having the papers available in the car would be far too simple. Resigned, she plunked her bag into her lap and gave up on trying to repair her look. She was a mess, and that was that.

"Don't you worry about inconveniencing me," she drawled. "It's not like I have a life."

Henry pulled into the snarl of traffic heading for Liberty and Wildon, while Zach sent her a speculative, sidelong glance. "Stroke of a pen gets you out of this any old time you want."

She determinedly shook her head. Much as she'd love to sever both their marital and business ties, if she let him off the hook, the man would fire her in the blink of an eye.

He leaned back in the leather seat, angling his body so that he faced her. "What if I promised you could keep your job?"

Rain rattled harder on the car's sunroof, while the wipers slapped their way across the windshield, blurring the view of the street.

Kaitlin made a half turn in the seat, meeting Zach's dark eyes. "That would require me trusting you."

"You can trust me," he assured her.

She coughed out a laugh. "You ruined my *life*."

He frowned. "I made you a very wealthy woman."

"I don't want to be a wealthy woman."

"I say again. You can get out of this anytime you want."

She made a show of glancing around the interior of the car. "Is there some way to exit this conversation?" she asked him. "Or does it just keep circling the drain?"

Horns honked in the lanes beside them as Henry inched his way through a left-hand turn. Kaitlin swiped at her damp, tangled hair, resisting an urge to slip off her soggy shoes and wiggle her toes into the thick carpet.

"You're going to find it very inconvenient being my business partner," Zach warned.

She cocked her head, watching him as she spoke. "Because you'll go out of your way to make it hell?"

He resettled himself in the butter-soft seat. "And here I thought I was being subtle."

"This is fifty pages long." Standing in the middle of Zach's penthouse living room, Kaitlin frowned as she leafed her way through the document.

"It deals with control of a multimillion-dollar corporation," he returned with what he hoped resembled patience. "We could hardly jot it down on a cocktail napkin."

Though he'd had a few days to come to terms with this bizarre twist in his life, Zach was still chafing at the circumstance. He didn't want to have to justify anything about Harper Transportation to Kaitlin, even temporarily. His grandma Sadie had complete faith in him—at least he'd always thought she'd had complete faith in him. He'd never had to explain anything about the company to her. He'd basically been running the show for over a decade.

But now there was Kaitlin. And she was underfoot. And she had questions. And he could only imagine what kind of monstrosity he'd be left with for an office building.

Dylan had pointed out yesterday that appeasing Kaitlin was better than losing half his company. Maybe it was. But barely.

"I'll need to have my lawyer look at this," Kaitlin announced, reaching down to pull open her oversize shoulder bag in order to deposit the document inside.

"Give it a read before you decide," Zach cajoled through half-gritted teeth. "It's not Greek." He pointed. "You and I sign page three, authorizing the board of directors. The board members have already signed page twenty, confirming my positions. The rest is…well, read it. You'll see."

She hesitated, peering at him with suspicion. But after a moment, she sighed, dropping her bag onto his sofa. "Fine. I'll take a look."

He tried not to cringe as her wet purse hit the white leather cushion of his new, designer Fendi.

"Your coat?" he offered instead, holding out his hands to accept it. The coat he'd hang safely in his hall closet before she had a chance to drape it over his ironwood table.

She slipped out of the dripping rain jacket, revealing a clingy, black-and-burgundy, knee-length dress. It had capped sleeves, a scooped neck and a pencil-straight skirt that flowed down to her shapely legs, which were clad in black stockings. Damp as they were, her high heels accentuated slim ankles and gorgeous calves.

Though they'd spoken briefly at the office this morning, she'd been wearing her coat at the time. He'd had no idea what was hidden beneath. Just as well he hadn't had *that* image inside his brain all day long.

"Thank you," she acknowledged, handing him the coat.

"I'm…uh…" He pointed in the general direction of the hallway and the kitchen, making his escape before she noticed he was ogling her body with his mouth hanging open.

In the kitchen, he found that his housekeeper had left a note informing him there was salad and a chicken dish in the fridge. She'd also left a bottle of Cabernet on the breakfast bar. Zach automatically reached for the corkscrew, breathing through the dueling emotions of frustration and arousal.

Sure, Kaitlin was an attractive woman. He knew that. He'd known that from the minute he met her. But there were attractive women everywhere. He didn't have to fixate on her.

He popped the cork.

No. No reason at all for him to fixate on her.

In fact, maybe he should get himself a date. A date would distract him. He'd been working too hard lately, that was all. A date with another, equally attractive woman would nip this fascination with Kaitlin in the bud.

He reached for the crystal glasses hanging from the rack below the cabinet.

Dylan had offered to introduce him to his newest helicopter pilot. He'd said she was attractive and athletic. She was a Yankees fan, but he could probably live with that. And she had a master's degree in art history. Who didn't like art history?

Before Zach realized what he'd done, he'd filled two glasses with wine.

"Oh, hell."

Then again, he supposed the woman deserved a drink. If she signed the papers, they'd toast the accomplishment. If she refused to sign, maybe the wine would loosen her up, and he could take another stab at convincing her.

He shrugged out of his suit jacket, moving farther down the

hallway to the master bedroom. There, he hung the jacket in his closet, shed his tie and glanced in the mirror above his dresser.

He definitely needed a shave. And his white shirt was wrinkled from being worn all day.

He glanced once at the jacket and considered putting it back on. But common sense prevailed. Instead, he unbuttoned his cuffs and rolled up the sleeves of his shirt. If this was a date, he'd shave and redress. But it wasn't a date. And his looks would be the last thing on Kaitlin's mind.

More comfortable, he returned to the kitchen and retrieved the wineglasses. He moved down the hallway to the living room. Inside the doorway, he paused.

Kaitlin seemed to have made herself at home. She'd kicked off her strappy shoes and curled her legs beneath her, knees bent and pressed together, stocking-clad feet pushing up against the arm of his sofa. Her hair was drying to a wild, glossy halo that framed her smooth skin. And her face was a study in concentration, red lips pursed, green eyes slightly squinted as she read her way through the pages.

She looked good in his living room, somehow settled and at home.

Funny, he'd seen her dressed up, dressed down, dancing with laughter and crackling with anger. But he'd never caught her unaware. And somehow he had the feeling this was the real woman, halfway between Vegas glitter and Saturday casual, her energy turned inward, mind working. He sensed a calm intelligence in her that he hadn't noticed before.

He must have moved, because she finally noticed him.

"Wine?" he offered, raising one of the glasses, walking forward, pretending he hadn't been staring.

"You're right," she told him, letting the papers drop into her lap, stretching an arm across the back of the sofa in an obviously unintended, sensual gesture.

"Never thought I'd hear you say that." But there was no bite to his words. He'd meant to mock her, but it came off as a gentle joke.

She flipped the document back to the first page and set it in front of her on the coffee table. "I'll sign it."

"Really?" Too late, he realized he sounded surprised. To cover, he handed her the glass of wine.

She accepted the glass and shrugged. "It's exactly what you said it was."

"How about that," he couldn't help but tease.

"Shocked the heck out of me," she returned, doing a double take, seeming to note he'd shed the jacket and tie.

He sat down on the other end of the couch. "Then, cheers." He lifted his glass.

She allowed a small smile, which made her prettier than ever. She leaned toward him, holding out her glass to clink it against his. The motion gave him a glimpse of her cleavage, and he was forced to drag his gaze away from her soft breasts.

They each took a sip.

Then her smile grew, and an impish dimple appeared in her right cheek. "Tough day at the office, dear?" She mimicked what was obviously a wifely voice of concern.

Something inside him responded warmly to the banter. "You know—" he paused for effect "—the usual."

"Is this weird?" she asked, eyes narrowing.

"Yes."

"Because it feels weird. I mean, on a scale of one to, well, weird, it's weird."

"Did that make sense inside your head?"

She took another drink, waving a dismissive hand. "I'm sure you got the gist of it."

"I did. And I agree. It's weird."

"We're married." She said the words in a tone of wonder.

"Yes, we are." Zach took a healthy swig from his own glass. He'd never been married. And even if he had, he couldn't help but doubt anything could prepare a man for this particular situation.

She paused, and then her voice went soft. "I'm not trying to ruin your life, you know."

He didn't like it that she seemed so vulnerable. It was better when she was acting tough and feisty. Then, it was easier to view her as a combatant. And he was beginning to admit fighting with Kaitlin was much safer than joking with her.

He struggled to put a hard note back in his voice. "I guess it was the blackmail scheme that had me confused."

Her green eyes were clear, open and honest. "I'm not looking to gain anything."

He made a show of skeptically raising his brows.

"I'm looking to set things right," she assured him.

He tried to sound doubtful. "Is that how this is playing out inside your head?"

"Once I've earned my way back into the good graces of my profession, you'll be home free. I want a career, Zach, not your company."

He had to admit, he believed her. He understood she was trying to make her own life better. Her methods weren't the most noble from where he was standing. But he did accept the fact that he was collateral damage.

She leaned forward and flipped to the signature page of the document. "Do you have a pen?"

"Sure." He rose and crossed to the small rosewood desk that held a telephone and a reading lamp.

"I'm meeting Lindsay for dinner," Kaitlin explained from behind him. "I don't want to be too late."

"I have a date," he lied, extracting a pen from the small desk drawer. He'd call Dylan and get the number of the pretty helicopter pilot just as soon as Kaitlin left.

"You're *cheating* on me?"

Her outburst surprised him, but when he turned, he saw the laughter lurking in her jade-green eyes.

"Yes," he answered easily, not about to rise to the bait. "I've been cheating on you since the wedding."

"Men," she huffed in pretend disgust, folding her arms across her chest, accenting her breasts.

Focusing beyond her lovely figure, he shrugged an apology on behalf of his gender as he crossed the room. "What can I say?"

She accepted the pen, bending her head to sign the papers. "Well, *I've* been faithful."

He waited for the punch line.

It didn't come.

"Seriously?" he asked.

She finished her signature with a flourish, declining to answer.

But he couldn't let it go. "You haven't had sex with anybody since Vegas?"

"What do you mean *since* Vegas." She sat up straight, handing the pen back in his direction. "Who do you think I had sex with in Vegas?"

He accepted it, feeling a twinge of remorse. "I didn't mean it that—"

"The only person I was with in Vegas was you and we didn't—" The amusement suddenly fled her eyes, replaced by uncertainty. "We, uh, didn't, did we?"

Okay, *this* was interesting. "You don't remember?" He might not have total recall of the entire night's events. But he knew they hadn't made love.

Then the vulnerability was back, and she slowly shook her head. "I barely remember the wedding."

He was tempted to string her along, but quickly changed his mind. The cursed vulnerability again. It made him want to protect her, not mess with her mind.

"We didn't," he assured her.

She tilted her head to one side. "Are you sure? Do *you* remember every minute?"

Their gazes locked for a couple of heartbeats.

"I'd remember that."

"So, you can't say for sure…"

"Has this been bothering you?" he asked.

"No."

"Because it sounds like—"

Suddenly, she snagged her bag and hooked it over her shoulder, coming to her feet. "It's not bothering me. If we did it, we did it."

"We *didn't*." Not that he hadn't wanted to. Not that he wouldn't love to. Not that he wasn't still—

Damn it. He had to stop going there.

"Because I'm not pregnant or anything," she said, slipping into her sexy shoes and straightening her clingy dress. The action pulled it tighter against her lithe body, and it was more than he could do not to let his gaze take a tour.

He summoned his strength. "Kaitlin. I think we need to leave Vegas back in Vegas."

"We tried."

That was true.

"But it didn't work," she pointed out.

"Blame Elvis," he drawled, fixing his gaze firmly on her face and telling himself to leave it right there.

Her smile grew. "You're funnier than you let on, you know?"

He gritted his teeth against her softening expression, those lips, those eyes, that tousled hair. It would be so easy to pull her into his arms and kiss her.

But for the first time in his life, he ignored the powerful urge.

"Thanks for signing the papers," he offered gruffly.

"Thanks for giving me a job."

The specter of her previous designs appeared inside his head. He didn't know what he'd do if she insisted on resurrecting them.

Now might not be the time. Then again, now might be the perfect time. They seemed to have come to a truce. Maybe he should take advantage of it.

"You know that building has been in my family for five generations," he declared.

"That doesn't mean it can't look good."

"There are a lot of different ways to make it look good." Classic ways. Functional ways. They were a transportation company, for goodness' sake, not an art museum.

He wished he could interest her in using the Hugo Rosche plans as a jumping-off point. Hugo had taken over after he'd canceled Hutton Quinn. Zach had paid a penalty to get out of the contract. But Hugo had left on good terms with a reference and several prospective clients set up by Zach. Hugo's plans made the most of the existing layout, and they'd only take about six months to implement.

"And I'm going to find the best one," she breezily promised. Her bravado frightened him.

"It's my heritage you're playing with, you know."

Her expression faltered for a split second, something close to pain flitting through her eyes. But she recovered instantly, and the confidence returned. "Then, you're a very lucky man, Zach Harper. Because I'm going to make your heritage a whole lot better."

Three

The following week, Kaitlin and Lindsay made their way into the bright pool of sunshine on the roof of the Harper Transportation building. The cement was solid beneath Kaitlin's feet, and the building seemed to fit seamlessly into its surroundings. Modern high-rises towered over on two sides, while across Liberty, they studied a row of dignified—if chipped—lion statues, and looked farther to the river.

The roof was square, blocked on one side by the service level and staircase. It was bordered by a three-foot-high concrete wall. Years of rain had stained it, but the mottled color evoked a certain nobility. Kaitlin couldn't help wonder what it would be like to work under the same roof as five generations of your ancestors.

Her mother had died when she was born. Her father was "unknown," not even a name on a birth certificate. And if nineteen-year-old Yvette Saville had had relatives somewhere nobody ever found them. All Kaitlin had of her own heritage was a single, frayed and blurry photo of her mother, and the

address of the rooming house where Yvette had been living prior
to Kaitlin's birth.

While her anger and frustration toward Zach had diminished
as the days went by, she couldn't seem to fight off the spurt of
jealousy that bubbled up when she thought about his heritage.
He'd had such a safe and privileged upbringing. While she was on
the outside looking in, he'd been wrapped in the loving embrace
of his wealthy family, wanting for nothing, experiencing the
finest life had to offer.

"Explain to me again why we couldn't go straight to Rundall's
for lunch?" called Lindsay. She'd fallen behind in her higher
heels and straight skirt.

"See that?" Kaitlin turned to walk backward, banishing her
negative thoughts as she swept her arm, pointing toward the deep
blue Hudson River. "If I can get a permit to add three stories,
the view will be amazing."

A steady hum of traffic rose up to meet them, while barges
slipped by against the tree-dotted New Jersey shoreline.

"Will that be expensive?" asked Lindsay, as she picked
her way across the rough surface, steadying herself against a
mechanical box, then an air-conditioning unit.

"Wildly," said Kaitlin, picturing the expanse of glass and the
marble floors.

Lindsay flashed a wide grin as she came abreast of Kaitlin
near the edge of the roof. "That's my girl. Not that Harper will
ever notice. The man has more money than God."

"It would seem," Kaitlin agreed, thinking back to the fine art
and antiques that decorated his huge penthouse apartment.

"I've been checking," said Lindsay in a conspiratorial tone,
swiping back her stray blond hairs in the freshening breeze. "Did
you know it started with the pirates?"

"What started with pirates?" Kaitlin peered over the edge to
the busy street below. She wished she had a scaffolding so she
could see exactly how the view would look if they went up three
stories.

"The Harper family wealth," Lindsay said. "Yo ho ho and a
bottle of rum. Pirates."

Kaitlin stretched up on her toes, shading her eyes against the brilliant sun. "I'm sure that's just a rumor."

New York City was full of colorful stories of countless founding families. Most of them were concocted by the families themselves to add social cachet and impress their friends. The Harpers could just as easily have been former potato farmers who arrived in the city from Idaho in 1910. Perhaps they'd sold something as mundane as farmland and crops to buy their first boat and start Harper Transportation.

"Of course it's a rumor," Lindsay pointed out. "It happened three hundred years ago. It's not like they have videotape."

Kaitlin cracked a smile at her friend's faux outrage. "Are you suggesting I've inherited tainted money?"

"I'm suggesting the man you're blackmailing was descended from thieves and murderers."

"Does that scare you?" Zach didn't scare Kaitlin anymore.

Well, not much. She was still intimidated by his angry glare. And she was definitely unsettled by the sexual awareness that bloomed to life whenever he strode by. It was becoming a regular part of her workday: email, coffee, drafting, Zach. Then boom, buzz, all she could think about was kissing him.

"Hell, no," Lindsay assured her. "I'm just sayin' you should watch out for his sword."

Kaitlin waggled her finger at Lindsay in admonishment. "That's a terrible joke."

Lindsay peered closer. "Are you blushing?"

"No," Kaitlin answered with a shake of her head, switching her attention to the steel gray barge plodding up the river.

"I didn't mean it the way it sounded."

"Sure you did."

Lindsay leaned forward to get a better view of Kaitlin's face. "You *are* blushing. What did I miss?"

"Nothing. I've barely seen him in three days."

Okay, so she'd seen him from afar, more than a few times. And he looked good from that distance—no frowns, no scowls. Her reaction to him was becoming almost comically predictable.

Her pulse rate would jump. Her skin would heat up. And she'd lose her train of thought.

"Are you falling for him?" asked Lindsay.

Kaitlin started to speak, but then stopped, unwilling to lie to Lindsay. "I'm admiring his features from afar," she admitted. "Along with half of the city."

Zach was an undeniably attractive man. So she found him good-looking? Big deal. So she occasionally found him charming? Another big deal.

He had breeding and education, and plenty of practice at dating and small talk. If she forgot about the fact that he'd tried to ruin her life, she could almost pretend he was a decent guy.

"He does make a hot pirate," Lindsay concurred with a saucy grin.

"Hot" definitely described the way he'd looked that night at his penthouse, his tie off, sleeves rolled up, a day's growth of beard shadowing his chin. He'd looked every inch the rakish pirate of his ancestors. And it had been more than sexy.

Lindsay was watching her closely. "Promise me you'll keep your head in the game."

Kaitlin tucked her loose hair firmly behind her ears, taking a quick check of her diamond stud earring. "My head is completely in the game," she assured Lindsay.

There wouldn't be a repeat of Vegas. Kaitlin had slipped up that night. She'd let down her guard, and Zach had turned on her within the week.

Apparently satisfied, Lindsay eased forward to peer over the edge. Taxis, buses and delivery trucks cruised past. Three city workers in hard hats set barriers up around an open manhole, while a police cruiser, lights flashing blue and red, pulled halfway up on the wide sidewalk.

"So, have you started unpacking yet?" asked Lindsay.

"Nope." Kaitlin watched two uniformed cops stride into a deli. She was more than happy to leave the topic of Zach behind. "I'm going to take advantage of having everything out of the way. Clean the carpets and paint the walls."

"Nesting?" asked Lindsay.

"Yes, I am." When she gave herself time to think about staying put in New York City, Kaitlin felt a surge of relief lighten her shoulders. She'd curled up in her window seat yesterday evening with a cup of cocoa, simply staring for an hour at the bustle of the neighborhood.

"You deserve a great place to call home," said Lindsay, warmth and caring evident in her tone.

Kaitlin smiled her agreement. "I may even buy that new rocker." She'd been admiring a big, overstuffed gliding rocker in the window of a local furniture store for a few months now. Something about it said home.

"You?" Lindsay teased. "A frivolous expenditure?"

Kaitlin nodded with conviction. With no means of support other than her part-time job, she'd been forced to be frugal during her college years. The habit was hard to break. But she was gainfully employed now, and she had good prospects. And she was determined to make herself a real home.

"First the rocker," she explained to Lindsay. "And then the Prestige espresso machine."

"I love hearing you talk like that." Lindsay laughed.

"It feels pretty good," Kaitlin admitted, then her voice caught on her age-old sensation of loneliness. "I *can* make it a real home."

Lindsay linked her arm and nudged up against her. "You've already made it a real home."

It didn't feel like a real home to Kaitlin. Then again, how would she know? Over her childhood years, most of her placements had been in group facilities instead of with families. The workers were mostly kind, but they came and went in shifts, and they often moved on to other jobs, replaced by new people, who were also nice, but also employees, not a family.

Lindsay gave her a squeeze, obviously recognizing that Kaitlin was getting emotional. "You ready for lunch?"

"Sure thing." There was no point in dwelling on the past. She was staying in New York City, and that was a great thing. The rocker would make a difference, she was sure of it. Maybe she'd get a cat, a calico or a black-and-white gerbil. A pet would make things that much more homey.

With one last look around, she followed Lindsay inside. They locked the rooftop door and took the aging elevator back to the third floor and Kaitlin's small office.

"There you are." Zach's greeting from inside the office sounded vaguely like an accusation.

"What are you doing here?" Kaitlin's guard immediately went up. She suspiciously scanned the room, the deck, the bookshelf, her computer, checking to see if anything had been disturbed. She'd put a password on her laptop, and she was keeping the preliminary renovation drawings under lock and key.

She'd made Zach promise to give her carte blanche on the project. But she still feared, given half a chance, he would try to micromanage it. She wasn't planning on giving him half a chance.

"I have something to show you," he announced from where he stood behind her tilted drafting table.

She saw that he'd rolled out a set of blue line drawings. She moved forward to get a better view. "Those aren't mine."

"They're something Hugo Rosche put together," he responded.

Kaitlin slipped between the desk and drafting table, while Lindsay waited in the doorway of the cramped office. Kaitlin stopped shoulder-to-shoulder with Zach, and he moved closer up against the wall.

"What's different than how it is now?" she asked, moving through the pages, noting that a few walls had been relocated. The lobby had been slightly expanded, and new windows were sketched in on the first floor.

"We'd also repaint, recarpet and get a decorator," said Zach.

She glanced up at him, searching his expression. "Is this a joke?"

He frowned at her.

"Because, I mean, if it's a joke, ha-ha." She dropped the pages back into place.

He looked affronted. "It's not a joke."

She gestured to the sheets of paper. "You're not seriously suggesting I use these."

"We don't need to make massive changes in order to improve the building," he insisted.

"I'm not a decorator, Zach. I'm an architect."

"Being an architect doesn't mean you need to tear down walls for the sake of tearing down walls."

She turned and propped her butt against the side of the desk, folding her arms over her chest and facing him head on. "Did you seriously think I'd fall for this?" Because if he had, he was delusional.

He lifted his chin. "I thought you'd at least consider it."

"I just considered it. I don't like it."

"Thank you so much for keeping such an open mind."

"Thank you so much for bringing me a fait accompli."

"I paid good money for these plans." He snagged the bottom of the sheets and began to roll them up. His voice rose, the offense clear in his tone. "And I paid good money for your original plans. And now I'm paying a third time for the same work."

Lindsay shifted forward, stepping fully into the room. "Would you prefer to fire Kaitlin and meet us in court?"

Zach's steel gaze shot her way.

He glared at her briefly, then returned his attention to Kaitlin. "I thought you could use them as a starting point."

Kaitlin shrugged. "Okay," she said easily.

His hands stilled. He drew back, eyes narrowing in suspicion. Then he paused and asked, "You will?"

She shrugged again. "Since they're virtually identical to the existing building, I've already used them as a starting point."

Lindsay coughed a surprised laugh.

Zach came back to life, snapping an elastic band around the paper roll, while Kaitlin hopped out of his way.

"It's my backup plan," Zach said to Dylan. It was Sunday afternoon, and the two men maneuvered their way through the crowded rotunda at Citi Field toward a Mets game. If there was one thing he'd learned from both his father and from Dylan's dad, it was that your contingencies had to have contingencies. Plans failed all the time. An intelligent man was prepared for failure.

Dylan counted on his fingers. "Plan A was to buy her off. Plan B was getting her to agree to the Hugo Rosche drawings. Low percentage on that one working, by the way." He skirted a trash can. "And now Plan C is to find her a new job?"

Zach didn't disagree on the Rosche drawings. It had been a long shot that she'd agree to use them. But finding her a new job could easily work. It was a well thought out strategy.

"She said it herself," he explained. "Her long-term goal is to get a good job. She wants her career back on track. And I don't blame her. Thing is, it doesn't have to be my building. It could be any building."

"She wants to stay in New York City," Dylan confirmed.

"New York City is a very big place. There are plenty of buildings to renovate."

"So, you invited her to the game, because…?"

That was another element of Zach's plan. "Because she was wearing a Mets T-shirt that day at her apartment. It turns out, she's a fan."

"And odds are she's never watched a game from a Sterling Suite," Dylan elaborated.

"I'm betting she hasn't," said Zach as he came to a stop near the escalator, glancing around for Kaitlin and Lindsay. "It works exceedingly well on Fortune 500 execs. Besides, my project is temporary. If I can find her a solid offer with a good firm, then she's got something permanent."

"And in order to accept the offer, she'll have to quit your project."

"Exactly." Zach couldn't help but smile at his own genius.

Dylan, on the other hand, had a skeptical expression on his face. "Good luck with that."

"Here she is," Zach announced in a loud voice, sending Dylan a quick warning glance.

The plan was perfectly sound. But it would take some finesse.

He wouldn't try to sell her on the idea of a new job right away. Today, he only wanted to smooth the path, get a little closer to her. He'd let her know he was interested in a good outcome for both of them. No reason they had to be at odds.

Next week, he'd make a few calls, talk to a few associates, field offers for her.

Kaitlin broke her way through the escalator lineup and angled toward them.

His mood lifted at the sight of her, and he recognized the danger in that hormonal reaction. It didn't mean he had a hope in hell of changing it. But it did mean he needed to be careful, keep his emotions in check and hold himself at a distance.

She was wearing a snug white T-shirt, faded formfitting blue jeans, scuffed white sneakers and a blue-and-orange Mets cap with a jaunty ponytail sticking out the back. He'd never had a girl-next-door thing, preferring glitz and glamour in his dates. But it didn't seem to matter what Kaitlin wore. She'd be his fantasy girl in a bathrobe.

Damn. He had to shut that image down right now.

Her friend Lindsay was a half pace behind her. She had topped a pair of black jeans with a white sleeveless blouse.

They came to a halt.

"Dylan," Zach said, resisting the urge to reach out and touch Kaitlin, "meet Kaitlin Saville and Lindsay Rubin."

"The lovely bride," Dylan teased Kaitlin, and Zach tensed at the edgy joke.

"The pirate," Lindsay countered with a low laugh, smoothly inserting herself between Dylan and Kaitlin, then shaking his hand.

"Zach's the pirate," Dylan informed her, a practiced smile masking his annoyance at what he considered an insulting label.

"I've been studying Zach's family history," Lindsay countered. "And I also came across yours."

"Why don't we head this way." Zach gestured toward the elevator. He didn't want an argument to mar the day. Plus, the game was about to start.

Kaitlin followed his lead, and she fell into step beside him.

"A pirate?" she asked him in what sounded like a teasing voice.

That was encouraging.

"So I'm told," he admitted.

"Well, that explains a lot."

Before Zach could ask her to elaborate, Lindsay's voice interrupted from behind. "It seems Caldwell Gilby cut a swath through the Spanish Main, plundering gold, ammunition and rum."

Zach could well imagine Dylan's affronted expression. The sparks were about to fly. But he had to admit, he kind of liked Lindsay's audacity.

"You can't trust everything you read on the internet," Dylan returned dryly.

Kaitlin leaned a little closer to Zach, voice lowering. "Is this going to end badly?"

"Depends," he answered, listening for the next volley.

"I read it in the *Oxford Historic Encyclopedia* at the NYU Library," came Lindsay's tart retort.

"It could end badly," Zach acknowledged.

While he'd long since accepted the fact that his family's wealth had its roots in some pretty unsavory characters, Dylan had always chosen to pretend his ancestor fought against the pirate Lyndall Harper, and on the side of justice.

The two men had zigzagged across the Atlantic for years, lobbing cannonballs at each other. They'd fought, that much was true. But neither was on the right side of the law.

The suite level elevator doors had opened, so they walked inside.

"Caldwell had letters of authority from King George," said Dylan, turning to face the glowing red numbers.

"Forged and backdated in 1804," Lindsay retorted without missing a bead.

"Have you ever seen the originals?" Dylan asked. "Because I've seen the originals."

Kaitlin merely grinned at Zach from beneath her ball cap. "My money's on Lindsay."

He took in her fresh face, ruby lips, dark lashes and that enticing little dimple. He caught the scent of coconut, and for a split second he imagined her in a bright bikini, flowers in her hair, on a tropical beach.

"Is it a bet?" she asked, interrupting his thoughts.

"Sorry?" He shook himself back to reality.

"Ten bucks says Lindsay wins." She held out her hand to seal the deal.

Zach took her small, soft hand in his, shaking slowly, drawing out the touch, his attraction to her buzzing through ever nerve cell in his body. "You're on."

The elevator came smoothly to a stop, and they made their way along the wide, carpeted hallway to the luxury suite. For many years, the Harpers and the Gilbys had shared a corporate suite for Mets games. Dylan's father used them the most often, but they had proven a valuable corporate tool for all of them in wooing challenging clients.

"Wow." The exclamation whooshed out of Kaitlin as she crossed through the arched entrance and into the big, balconied room. It comfortably held twenty. A waiter was setting out snacks on the countertop bar, next to an ice-filled pail of imported beer and a couple of bottles of fine wine.

"Will you look at this." Like an excited kid, she beelined across to the open glass doors and out onto the breezy, tiered balcony, where two short rows of private seats awaited them.

Happy to leave Dylan and Lindsay to their escalating debate, Zach followed Kaitlin out.

"So this is how the other half lives," she said, bracing her hands on the painted metal rail, and gazing out over home plate. Rows of fan-filled seats cascaded below them, and a hum of excitement wafted through the air.

"It works well for entertaining clients." Zach heard a trace of apology in his voice, and he realized he wanted her to know it wasn't all about self-indulgence.

"At Shea Stadium, we used to sit over there." She pointed to the blue seats high behind third.

"Was that when you were a kid?"

She shook her head. "It was when we were in college." And a wistful tone came into her voice. "My first live game was sophomore year."

"So, you were a late bloomer?" He shifted to watch her profile, wondering what had prompted the sadness.

"As a kid, I watched as many as I could on TV." She abruptly turned to face the suite, and her tone went back to normal. "You got any beer in there?"

"No live games as a kid?" he persisted, seeing an opening to get to know her on a more personal level.

"Not a lot of money when I was a kid." She sounded defiant. He could tell he was being dared to probe further.

He opened his mouth to ask, but a cheer came up from the crowd as the players jogged onto the field.

Kaitlin clapped her hands. And by the time the din had abated, Zach decided to leave it alone. He patted one of the balcony chairs in the front row. "Have a seat. I'll bring you a beer." Two stairs up, he twisted back. "You want chips or something?"

"Hot dog?" she asked.

He couldn't help but grin at the simple request. "One hot dog, coming up."

Back inside the suite, while Dylan explained some of the finer points of King George's Letters of Authority, the waiter quickly organized hot dogs and beer.

In no time, Zach was settled next to Kaitlin, and the game was under way.

As the Mets went up to bat, they ate their loaded hot dogs. Between bites, she unselfconsciously cheered for the hits and groaned at the strikes. Zach found himself watching her more than he watched the players.

After the final bite of her hot dog, she licked a dab of mustard from the pad of her thumb. The gesture was both subconscious and sexy. Somehow, it looked remarkably like a kiss.

"That was delicious," she said, grinning around the tip of her thumb. "Thanks."

He tried to remember the last time he'd dated a woman who enjoyed the simple pleasure of a hot dog. Lobster, maybe, caviar, certainly, and expensive champagne was always a winner. But the finer things had mattered to his dates, his money had always mattered.

Then he remembered Kaitlin owned half his fortune. And he remembered they weren't on a date.

"So…" She adjusted her position, crossing one leg over the opposite knee, and adjusted her cap, apparently remembering the same things as him. "Why did you invite me here?"

He feigned innocence. "What do you mean?"

She gestured to the opulence behind them. "The suite. The baseball game. Imported beer. What's up?"

"We're working together."

"And…" She waited.

"And I thought we should get to know each other." Sure, he had another objective. But it was perfectly rational for the two of them to get to know each other. The renovations would take months. They'd be in each other's lives for quite some time to come.

"I'm not signing the divorce papers," she warned him.

"Did I ask?" There was no need for her to get paranoid.

"And I'm not changing the renovation designs, either."

"You could at least let me look at them."

"No way," she determinedly stated.

He tried feigning nonchalance. "Okay. Then let's talk about you."

She came alert. "What about me?"

"What are your plans? I mean long-term. Not just this single project."

The crack of a bat against the ball resonated through the stadium, and she turned to face forward while a runner sprinted to first. "That's no secret," she answered, gaze focused on the game. "A successful career in architecture. In New York City."

He took a sip of the cold beer, concentrating on getting this conversation just right. "I'd like to help you."

Her mouth quirked into a rueful smile. "You are helping. Reluctantly, we both know. But you *are* helping."

"I mean in addition to the Harper renovation project. I know people. I have contacts."

"I'm sure you do." She kept her attention fixed on the game while the opposing pitcher threw a strike, retiring the batter, and the Mets headed out to the field.

"Let me use them," Zach offered.

She turned then to paste him with a skeptical stare. "Use your contacts? To help *me?*"

"Yes," he assured her with a nod.

She thought about it for a few minutes while the pitcher warmed up. Zach was tempted to prompt her, but he'd messed up so many conversations with her already, he decided silence was the safer route.

"I read where you're going to the chamber of commerce dinner next Friday," she finally ventured, turning to watch him.

"The resurgence of global trade in northern Europe," he confirmed. They'd asked him to speak. He'd prefer to sit in the back and enjoy the single malt, but having a profile at these things was always good for business.

"Are you taking anyone?" she asked, gaze darting back to the action on the field.

"You mean a date?"

She nodded. "It's a dinner. I assume it would be partly social. It seems to me it would be acceptable to bring a date."

"Yes, it's acceptable. And no, I don't have one."

Another batter cracked a high fly ball. They watched the trajectory until it was caught out in center field.

"Will you take me?"

Zach rocked back and turned. A reflexive rush of excitement hit his body as he studied her profile. "You're asking me for a date?"

But she rolled her eyes and adjusted her cap. "I'm asking you to get me in the door, Zach, not dance with me. You said you wanted to help. And there will be people there who are good for my career."

"Right." He shifted in his seat, assuring himself he wasn't disappointed. It was a lie, of course. But he definitely wasn't stupid.

Dating Kaitlin would be a huge mistake. Dancing with her was out of the question. What if it was as great as he'd remembered? What then?

She drew a satisfied sigh, her shoulders relaxing. "And, before Friday, if you wouldn't mind telling at least five people that you've hired me back. Influential people. It would be great for me if word got around."

He had no right to be disappointed. This was business for her. It was business for him, too. Introducing her around at the chamber dinner played right into Plan C. She was right. There would be influential people there, a myriad of corporate executives, many of whom would have contacts in the architectural world. If he was lucky, really lucky, she'd find a job right there at the dinner.

Still, he struggled to keep his voice neutral as he told her, "Sure. No problem."

"You did offer to help," she pointed out.

"I said sure."

"Are you annoyed?" she asked.

"I'm being blackmailed," he reminded her. Was he supposed to be thrilled about it?

"Every marriage has its complications," she returned on an irreverent grin.

Just then, the Mets pitcher struck out the third batter with the bases loaded, and Kaitlin jumped from her seat to cheer.

Zach watched her in the sunlight and struggled very hard to feel annoyed. But then she punched a fist in the air, and her T-shirt rode up, revealing a strip of smooth skin above her waistband. And annoyance was the last thing he was feeling toward his accidental wife.

The chamber dinner was a dream come true for Kaitlin. The people she met were friendly and professional, and she came away feeling as if she'd met the who's who of the Manhattan business world. Zach had certainly stuck to his pledge of helping her. He'd introduced her to dozens of potential contacts, left her in interesting conversations, but seemed to magically appear whenever she felt alone or out of place.

It was nearly midnight when they finally climbed aboard his thirty-foot yacht for the return trip to Manhattan. Like the suite at the baseball game, the yacht clearly showed Zach had the means and the desire to enjoy the finer things in life. Lindsay was right, Kaitlin could spend as much as she needed on the renovations, and he'd barely notice.

The chamber dinner had been held at an island marina just off the coast of southern Manhattan. Most people had traveled by water taxi but a few, like Zach, had brought their own transportation.

"This is a nice ride," she acknowledged one more time, as they settled into a grouping of comfortable, white, cushioned furniture. The sitting area, on a teak wood deck, was positioned next to a covered hot tub near the stern of the boat, protected from the wind by a glass wall at midship, but providing an incredible view over the aft rail.

Kaitlin chose a soft armchair, while Zach took a love seat at a right angle to her, facing the stern. The pilot powered up the engine, and they glided smoothly out into the bay.

"It's slower than a helicopter," said Zach. "But I like it out here at night."

Kaitlin tipped her head and gazed at the twinkling skyline. A three-quarter moon was rising, and a few stars were visible beyond the city's glow. "You have a helicopter?"

"Dylan has the helicopters. My company owns ships."

Kaitlin had liked Dylan, even if Lindsay hadn't seemed to warm up to him. Then again, there were few things Lindsay enjoyed more than a rollicking debate, and Dylan had played right into her hand. Kaitlin was convinced Lindsay missed being in a courtroom. Lindsay had worked for a year as a litigator, and Kaitlin had always wondered about her choice to take the teaching position.

"Tell me more about the pirates," she said to Zach. She'd never met anyone with such a colorful family history.

"You want a drink or anything?" he asked.

She shook her head, slipping off her shoes and bending her knees to tuck her feet beneath her in the shimmering black cocktail dress. "One more glass of champagne, and I'll start singing karaoke."

"Champagne it is." He started to rise, his devilish smile showing straight white teeth in the muted deck light.

"Don't you dare," she warned, with a waggle of her finger. "Trust me. You do not want me to sing."

He rocked back into his seat and loosened his tie. He ran a hand, spread-fingered, through his thick hair and crossed one ankle over the opposite knee. In the buffeting breeze, with the faint traces of fatigue around his dark eyes, he looked disheveled and compellingly sexy.

"Back to the pirates," she prompted in an effort to distract herself from her burgeoning desire. "Is it all true?"

He shrugged easily. "Depends on what you've heard."

"I heard that your ancestor was a pirate, arch enemy of Dylan's ancestor, and the two of them formed a truce nearly three hundred years ago on what is now Serenity Island. I heard the nexus of your fortune is stolen treasure."

Criminal or not, she still found herself envious of his detailed family history. Zach would know details of his parents, his grandparents, his aunts and uncles, and every ancestor back three hundred years. Kaitlin would give anything to be able to go back even one generation.

"Well, it's all true," said Zach. "At least as far as we can tell. Dylan's in denial."

Kaitlin laughed lightly, remembering the argument at the baseball game. "It sure sounded like it."

Zach removed his tie and tossed it on the love-seat cushion beside him. "Dylan wants to pretend his family was pure of heart. I think he must have more scruples than me."

"You're unscrupulous?" she couldn't resist asking.

"Some would say."

"Would they be right?"

He looked her square in the eyes. "Like I'm going to answer that."

She couldn't tell if he was still teasing. And maybe that was deliberate. "Are you trying to keep me off balance?" she asked, watching his expression closely.

"You're not exactly on my side."

"I thought we'd formed a truce." She certainly felt as if they'd formed a truce tonight.

"I'm appeasing you," he told her. His tone and dark eyes were soft, but the words revealed his continued caution.

"And I'm trying to build you a masterpiece," she responded tartly.

He sighed, and seemed to relax ever so slightly. "You're trying to build yourself a masterpiece."

She had to concede that one. Her primary motivation in this was her own reputation. Of course, it was all his fault she was forced into this position.

"You make a fair point," she admitted.

"So, who's unscrupulous now?"

"I'm not unscrupulous. Just practical." She had no one in this world to depend on but herself.

Orphans learned that fact very quickly in life. If she didn't have a career, if she couldn't provide for herself, nobody would do it for her. Since she was old enough to understand, she'd feared poverty and loneliness.

She was sure the view was quite different from where Zach was sitting on millions of dollars worth of New York real estate. He had a successful company, money to burn and a lineage that went back to the dawn of statehood.

"So, what have you decided?" he asked.

"About what?" Was there anything left outstanding on their deal? She thought they were both quite clear at this point.

"My building. You've been working at it for a couple of weeks now. Tell me what you have in mind."

Kaitlin instantly saw through his ploy. No wonder he'd

behaved so well this evening. He'd been lulling her into a false send of security.

She came to her feet, keeping a close eye on him, backing toward the rail. The teak deck was cool and smooth beneath her bare feet. "Oh, no, you don't. I'm not opening myself up for a fight over the details."

He rose with her. "You'll need my input at some point. It might as well be—"

"Uh-uh." The breeze brushed the filmy, scalloped-hem dress against her legs and whipped the strands of hair that had worked their way loose from her updo. "No input. *My* project."

He widened his stance. "I'll have to approve the final designs."

The waves rolled higher, and she braced herself against the rail. "What part of carte blanche didn't you understand?"

He took a few steps forward. "The part where I sign the check."

"*We* sign the check."

He came even closer, all pretense of geniality gone from his expression. He was all business, all intimidation. "Right. And 'we' had best be happy with both the plans and the price tag."

"There is no limit on this project's budget."

He came to a halt, putting a hand on the rail, half trapping her. "I won't let you bankrupt my company."

She struggled not to react to his nearness. "Like I could possibly bankrupt Harper Transportation. You give me too much credit."

The boat lunged into a trough, and he swayed closer. "You want to see the balance sheets?"

"I want to see a new Manhattan skyline."

"It's talk like that that scares me, Kaitlin."

Her scare him?

He was the one unsettling her.

His intense expression brought her heart rate up. His lips were full, chin determined, eyes intense, and his hard, rangy body was far too close for her comfort. Sweat prickled at her hairline, formed between her breasts, gathered behind her knees, and was then cooled by the evening breeze.

His arms were only inches away. He could capture her at any moment, kiss her, ravage her.

She swallowed against her out-of-control arousal.

Any second now, she'd be throwing herself in his arms. Maybe talking about the renovation was the lesser of all evils.

"I was planning more light." Her voice came out sexy, husky, and she couldn't seem to do a thing about it. "More glass. A higher lobby. Bigger offices."

Had he moved closer?

"Bigger offices mean fewer offices," he pointed out.

She didn't disagree.

"Do you know the cost of space in midtown Manhattan?" His rebuke sounded like a caress.

"Do you know the soft value of impressing your future clients?" she returned, her brain struggling hard to grasp every coherent thought.

Had *she* moved closer? Her nose picked up his scent, and it was sensually compelling. She swore she could feel the heat of his body through his dress shirt.

"Do you think the makers of tractor parts and kitchen appliances care what my lobby looks like?" His breath puffed against her lips.

"Yes."

They stared at each other in silence, inhaling and exhaling for long seconds. The rumble of the yacht's motor filled the space around them.

Something dangerous flared in Zach's intense gray eyes. It was darkly sensual and completely compelling.

Her body answered with a rush of heat and a flare of longing that sent a throbbing message to every corner of her being.

She struggled through the muddle of emotions clouding her brain. "The people who make tractor parts also have tickets to Lincoln Center. They do care about your lobby."

"It's a building, not a piece of art." The yacht lurched, and his hand brushed against hers. She nearly groaned out loud.

"It can be both," she rasped.

Things could do double duty.

Look at Zach. He was both an adversary and a—

What? What was she saying?

He could be her lover?

"Kaitlin?" His voice was strangled, while his gaze flared with certain desire. His full lips parted, his head tipping toward hers.

The boat rolled on a fresh set of waves, and she gripped the rail, transfixed by the sight of his body closing in on hers.

She flashed back to Vegas.

He'd kissed her there.

How could she have ever doubted it?

Elvis had pronounced them husband and wife, and Zach had thrown his arms around her, kissing her thoroughly and endlessly. It was only the cheers from the crowd that had finally penetrated their haze and forced them to pull apart. It was a miracle they hadn't slept together that night.

Why hadn't they slept together that night?

She remembered getting into the elevator with a couple of her female coworkers, then stumbling into her room and dropping, fully dressed, onto the plush, king-size bed.

No Zach.

But he was here now.

And they were alone.

And she remembered. She wished she didn't. But she remembered his lips on hers, his arms around her, the strength of his embrace, the taste of his mouth, the sensual explosions that burst along her skin.

She wanted it again, wanted it so very, very much.

She gave in to her desire and leaned ever so slightly forward. His mouth instantly rushed to hers. His free arm snaked around her, pressing against the small of her back, pulling her tight as the deck surged beneath them.

She pressed forward, arms twining around his neck. Her lips softened, parted. He murmured her name, and his hand splayed farther down her spine. His tongue invaded, and the taste of him combined with the scent of the salt air, the undulation of the boat and heat of his hands brought a moan from her very core.

He shifted so that his back was to the rail. His free hand caressed her cheek, brushed through her hair, moved down to her neck, her shoulder. He pushed off the strap of her dress, then his lips followed, tasting their way along her bare, sensitized skin.

His kisses, his passion, made her gasp. She tangled her fingers through his hair, pushing her body tightly against his, shifting her thighs as his leg slipped between them. His hand cupped her breast through the flimsy fabric of her dress, while his lips found hers again, and she bent backward with the exquisite pressure of his hot kiss.

The boat lurched again, and they lost their balance, stumbling a few steps sideways.

Zach was quick to steady her, clasping her tightly to him, lips next to her ear.

"You okay?" His voice was hollow.

"I'm—" She drew a shaky breath.

Was she okay? What on earth had she just done? One minute they were arguing over office sizes, the next they were practically attacking each other.

He held her tight. Neither spoke as they drew deep breaths. Finally, he stroked her messy hair. "Are you thinking what I'm thinking?"

"That we've both gone completely insane?"

He chuckled low. "That's pretty close."

"We can't do this."

"No kidding."

"You need to let go of me."

"I know." He didn't move.

"I'm blackmailing you. You're trying to outflank, outmaneuver and outthink me along the way. And then we're getting divorced."

"As long as we're both clear on the process."

The flutter in her stomach told her there was way more to it than that. But she had to fight it. She couldn't let herself be attracted to this man. She certainly couldn't let herself kiss him, or worse.

They were adversaries. And this was her one chance to get her life back. And she couldn't let any lingering sexual desire mess that up.

"You need to let me go, Zach."

Four

After a long, sleepless night, and a lengthy heart-to-heart with Lindsay as they drove up the coast of Long Island, Kaitlin watched her friend browse through a tray of misshapen silver coins in a small beachfront antique shop.

"I never thought I'd hear myself say this." Lindsay selected one plastic-wrapped item and read the provenance typed neatly on the attached card. "But, as your lawyer, I must strongly advise you not to sleep with your husband."

"I am *not* sleeping with my husband," Kaitlin reminded her. And she had absolutely no intention of going there. Desire and action were two completely different things.

Two women checking out a painting in the next aisle slid their curious gazes to Kaitlin, and their expressions shifted from smirks to bemusement.

Kaitlin leaned a little closer to Lindsay and whispered, "Okay, that just sounds stupid when I say it out loud."

"He's playing you," said Lindsay, dropping the first coin and switching to another, turning it over to read.

"Neither of us meant for it to happen," Kaitlin pointed out. Zach's shock and regret had seemed as genuine as hers.

Lindsay glanced up from the coin, arching her a skeptical look. "Are you sure about that?"

"I'm sure," Kaitlin returned with conviction. They'd both sworn not to let it happen again. It was as much her fault as his.

"And what were you doing right before you kissed him?" Lindsay gave up on the coin rack and meandered her way across the shop floor.

Kaitlin followed, only half paying attention to the merchandise. Lindsay was the one who'd suggested driving up the coast to visit antique stores. They'd never done it before, but Kaitlin was game for anything that would distract her.

"We were on deck," she told Lindsay. "Fantastic boat, by the way."

"You mentioned that. So, were you eating? Drinking? Stargazing?"

"Arguing art versus architecture." Kaitlin took her mind back to the first minutes of the return trip. "He wanted to see my designs."

"I rest my case." Lindsay lingered in front of a glass case displaying some more gold coins. "Aha. This is what I was looking for."

"What case?" asked Kaitlin. What was Lindsay resting?

Lindsay fluttered a dismissive hand, attention on the coins. "The case against Zach." Then she tapped her index finger against the glass in answer to a clerk's unspoken question. "I'd like to see that one."

"I don't follow," said Kaitlin.

"The coin is from the *Blue Glacier*."

"Yes, it is," the clerk confirmed with an enthusiastic smile, unlocking the case and extracting a plastic-covered, gold, oblong coin.

"You were resting your case," Kaitlin prompted.

Lindsay inspected the coin, holding it up to the sunlight and turning it one way, then the other. "You were arguing with Zach about art versus architecture. Which side were you on, by the way?"

"Zach's afraid my renovation plans will be impractical," explained Kaitlin. "I told him architecture could be both beautiful and functional. He's stone-cold on the side of function."

"Not hard to tell that from his building." Lindsay put down her purse and slipped the coin under a big magnifying glass on a stand on the countertop.

"When did you become interested in coins?" asked Kaitlin. Lindsay was going through quite a procedure here.

"The two of you were fighting," Lindsay continued while she peered critically at the coin. "I'm assuming you were winning since, aside from holding all the trump cards, you were right." She straightened. "Then suddenly, poof, he's kissing you."

The clerk eyed Kaitlin with obvious interest, while Lindsay gave Kaitlin a knowing look. "Do you think there's a slim possibility it was a distraction? Do you think, maybe, out of desperation to seize control of the project, your *husband* might be trying to emotionally manipulate you?"

Kaitlin blinked. Manipulate her?

"You know," Lindsay continued, "if you gave away the fact you thought he was hot—"

"I never told him he was hot."

"There are other ways to give yourself away besides talking. And you *do* think he's hot."

The clerk's attention was ping-ponging between the two women.

Kaitlin realized she probably *had* given herself away. On numerous occasions. And while they were arguing on the boat, her attraction to Zach must have been written all over her face.

But what about Zach? Had he felt nothing? Could he actually be that good an actor? Had he pounced on an opportunity?

Humiliation washed over her. Lindsay was right.

"Darn it," Kaitlin hissed under her breath. "He was *faking?*"

Lindsay patted her arm in sympathy, her tone going gentle. "That'd be my guess."

Kaitlin scrunched her eyes shut.

"I'll take this one," Lindsay told the clerk. Then she wrapped a bracing arm around Kaitlin's shoulders. "Seriously, Katie. I hate to be the one to say this. But what are the odds he's falling for you?"

Lindsay was right. She was so, so right. Kaitlin had been taken in by a smooth-talking man with an agenda. He didn't want her. He wanted her architectural designs, so he could shoot holes in them, talk her out of them, save himself a bundle of money. His interests were definitely not Kaitlin's interests.

How could she have been so naive?

She clamped her jaw and took a bracing breath.

Then she opened her eyes. "You're right."

"Sorry."

"Don't sweat it. I'm fine," Kaitlin huffed. She caught a glimpse of the hefty price tag on the coin and seized the opportunity to turn the attention from herself. "You know that's two thousand dollars?"

"It's a bargain," said the clerk, punching keys on the cash register.

But Lindsay wasn't so easily distracted. "I think he's trapped. I think he's panicking. And I think *he* thinks you'll be more malleable if you fall for him."

"How long have you been interested in antique coins?" Kaitlin repeated. Notwithstanding her desire to change the subject, it really *was* a lot of money.

"I'm not interested in coins," Lindsay replied. "I'm interested in pirates."

Oh, this was priceless. "You're fixating on Dylan Gilby?"

"Wrong. I'm fixating on *Caldwell* Gilby. I'm proving that smug, superior Dylan does, indeed, owe his wealth to the ill-gotten gains of his pirate ancestor."

"The *Blue Glacier was* sunk by pirates," the clerk offered as she accepted Lindsay's credit card to pay for the purchase.

"By the *Black Fern*," Lindsay confirmed in a knowledgeable and meaningful tone. "Captained by dear ol' Caldwell Gilby."

The clerk carefully slid the coin in a velvet pouch embossed with the store's logo. "The captain of the *Blue Glacier* tried to scuttle the ship against a reef rather than give up his cargo. But the pirates got most of it anyway. A few of the coins were recovered from the wreck in 1976." The clerk handed Lindsay the pouch. "You've made a good purchase."

As they turned for the door to exit the pretty little shop, Lindsay held up the pouch in front of Kaitlin's face. "Exhibit A."

Kaitlin searched her friend's expression. "You have got to get back in the courtroom."

"Weren't we talking about you?" asked Lindsay. "Kissing your husband?"

"I don't think so." Kaitlin was going to wallow through that one in private.

Lindsay dropped the coin into her purse and sobered. "I don't want you getting hurt in all this."

Kaitlin refused to accept that. "I'm not about to get hurt. I kissed him. Nothing more." That was, of course, the understatement of the century.

Still, they'd come to their senses before anything serious had happened. Or maybe Kaitlin was the one who'd come to her senses. Zach hadn't been emotionally involved on any level. Even now, he was probably biding his time, waiting for the next opportunity to manipulate her all over again.

"He's only after one thing," Lindsay declared with authority.

Kaitlin struggled to find the black humor. "And it's not even the usual thing."

Lindsay gave Kaitlin's shoulder another squeeze. "Just don't let your heart get caught in the crossfire."

"My heart is perfectly safe. I'm fighting for my career." Kaitlin wouldn't get tripped up again. She couldn't afford it. She was fighting against someone who was even less principled than she'd ever imagined.

Dylan showed his disagreement, backing away from Zach's office desk. "I am *not* stealing corporate secrets for you."

Zach exhaled his frustration. "They're my corporate secrets. You're not stealing them, because I *own* them."

"That's the Harper family style," Dylan sniffed in disdain. "Not the Gilbys'."

"Will you get off your moral high horse." It was all well and good for Dylan to protect his family name, but it had gotten completely out of hand the past few weeks.

"I have principles. So, sue me."

"I give you the key to my car." Zach ignored Dylan's protests and began to lay out a simple, straightforward plan.

Dylan folded his arms belligerently across the front of his business suit. "So I can break in to it."

"So you can *unlock* it. There is no breaking required."

"And steal Kaitlin's laptop."

"Her briefcase is probably a better bet," Zach suggested. "I suspect the laptop has a password. You photocopy the drawings. You put them back. You lock my trunk, and you're done."

"It's stealing, Zach. Plain and simple."

"It's photocopying, Dylan. Even Kaitlin's pit bull of a lawyer—"

"Lindsay."

Zach rapped his knuckles on his desktop. "Even Lindsay would have to admit that intellectual property created by Kaitlin while she was on the Harper Transportation payroll belongs to the company. And the company belongs to me."

"And to her."

Zach, exasperated, threw up his hands. "Whose side are you on?"

"This doesn't feel right."

Zach glared at his lifelong friend, searching for the argument that would bring Dylan around to logic. He couldn't help but wish a few of Caldwell's more disreputable genes had trickled down through the generations.

It wasn't as if they were knocking over a bank. It was nothing more than a frat prank. And he owned the damn designs. And while they might technically be half hers, they were also half his—morally, they were all his—and he had a corporation to protect. A corporation that employed thousands of people, all of them depending on Zach to make good decisions for Harper Transportation.

"I need to know she won't ruin me," he said to Dylan. "We know she's out for revenge. And think about it, Dylan. If she was only worried we'd disagree on the aesthetics of the renovation, she'd flaunt the drawings in my face. She's up to something."

Dylan stared in silence for a long minute, and Zach could almost feel him working through the elements of the situation.

"Up to what?" he finally asked, and Zach knew he had him.

"Up to spending Harper Transportation into a hole we can't climb out of then walking away and letting me sink."

"You think she'd—"

"I *don't know* what she'd do. That's my point. I don't know anything about this woman except that she blames me for everything that's wrong in her life."

Even as he said the words to Dylan, Zach was forced to silently acknowledge they weren't strictly true. He knew more than that about Kaitlin. He knew she was beautiful, feisty and funny. He knew her kisses made him forget they were enemies. And he knew he wanted her more than he'd ever wanted any woman in his life.

But that only meant he had to be tougher, even more determined to win. His feelings for her were a handicap, and he had to get past them.

"If it was you," Zach told Dylan in complete honesty, "if someone was after you, I'd lie, cheat and steal to save you."

Dylan hesitated. "That's not fair."

"How is it not fair?"

"You'd lie, cheat and steal at the drop of a hat."

Zach couldn't help but grin. It was a joke. Dylan had no basis for the accusation, and they both knew it.

Zach rounded the desk, knowing Dylan was on board. "That's because I'm a pirate at heart."

"And I am not."

Zach clapped Dylan on the shoulder. "But I'm working on you."

"That's what scares me."

"You may be a lot of things," said Zach, "but scared isn't one of them."

Dylan shook his head in both disgust and capitulation. "Give me your damn car keys," he grumbled. "And you owe me one."

Zach extracted his spare key from his pocket and handed them to Dylan. "I'll pay it back anytime you want. We'll be at Boondocks in an hour. The valet parking is off Forty-fourth."

Dylan glanced down at the silver key in his palm. "How did it come to this?"

"Lately, I ask myself that every morning."

Dylan quirked a half smile. "Maybe if you'd get yourself back on the straight and narrow."

"I am on the straight and narrow. Now get out there and steal for me."

Dylan on side, Zach cleared his evening's schedule and exited his office, making his way to the third floor. He had been making a point by putting Kaitlin in such a cramped space. It occurred to him that Dylan might be right. His moral compass could, in fact, be slipping.

He wasn't particularly proud of this next plan. But he didn't see any other way to get the information. And the situation was getting critical. Finding Kaitlin a new job wasn't going as smoothly as he'd expected. There was the real possibility he'd have to implement her renovation plans, and he couldn't afford to be blindsided by whatever extravagant and ungainly design she'd dreamed up.

He arrived at her office as she was locking the door at the end of the workday. She had both her laptop and a burgundy leather briefcase in her hands.

"You busy for dinner?" he asked without preamble.

She turned in surprise, her gaze darting up and down the hall, obviously worried about who might see them talking.

"Why?" Suspicion was clear in her tone.

"I'm attending a business event," he offered levelly.

"On your yacht?"

He tried to interpret her expression. Were her words a rebuke or a joke? Was she nervous at the thought of being alone with him again? If so, could it be because she was still attracted to him?

They'd pledged to keep their hands off each other, but she could be wavering. He was definitely wavering. He'd been wavering as soon as the words were out of his mouth.

"At Boondocks," he answered, shelving his physical desire for the moment. "I thought you might like to meet Ray Lambert."

Her green eyes widened. Ah, now he had her attention.

Ray Lambert was president of the New York Architectural Association. Zach had done his homework on this. He'd planned an introduction so valuable, it would be impossible for Kaitlin to say no to dinner.

"You're meeting Ray Lambert?" she asked cautiously.

"For dinner. Him and his wife."

Now her tone was definitely wary as she tried to gauge his motives. "And you're willing to take me along?"

Zach gave a careless shrug. "If you don't want to—"

"No, I want to." Her brow furrowed. "I'm just trying to figure out your angle."

He couldn't help but admire the way her brain was working through this. She was smart. But he was smarter. At least in this instance. With anybody but Ray Lambert, the plan would likely have failed.

"My angle is meeting your conditions for returning my company to me," Zach told her. It was true. It wasn't the whole truth, but it was part of the truth. "You want a career in this town, Ray's a good guy to meet."

She tilted her head to an unconsciously sexy angle. "No strings attached?"

His gaze automatically dropped to her luscious lips and his primal brain engaged. He didn't intend to lower his voice to a sexy timbre, nor did he plan to ease his body forward, but it all happened anyway. "What kind of strings did you have in mind?"

"You promised," she reminded him, looking trapped and worried.

"So did you."

"I'm not doing anything."

"I'm not doing anything, either," he lied. He was thinking plenty, and his body was telegraphing his desire. "Your imagination's filling in the blanks."

"You're looking at me," she accused.

"You're looking back," he countered.

"Zach."

"Katie." It was a stupid move, and not at all in keeping with his grand plan for tonight, but he reached forward and brushed his knuckles up against hers. It was a subtle touch, but it had the impact of a lightning bolt.

It obviously hit her, too. And he couldn't stop the surge of male satisfaction that overtook his body.

Her cheeks flushed, her irises deepened to emeralds. Her voice went sultry. "This isn't a date."

"Don't trust yourself?" he dared.

"I don't trust *you*."

"Smart move," he conceded, admiring her intelligence all over again as he pulled back from his brinkmanship.

He knew Harper Transportation had to be his primary concern. And he needed to get his hands on her drawings by fair means or foul. His company, his employees, his family legacy, all depended on it.

"Are you trying to make me say no?" she asked him.

"I honestly don't know what I'm trying to do." The confession was out of him before he could censor it.

Complicated didn't begin to describe his feelings for Kaitlin. He desperately wanted to kiss her. He craved the feel of her body against his. Given half a chance, he knew he'd tear off her clothes and make love to her until neither of them could move.

And then the power balance would be completely in her favor, and Harper Transportation wouldn't stand a chance.

He forced himself to back off farther, putting a buffer of space between them.

"Ray Lambert?" she confirmed, apparently willing to put up with Zach for the introduction.

He gave her a nod. Despite the detour into their inconvenient attraction to one another, his plan had worked. As he'd known it would. The intellectual evaluation of another person's emotions was an astonishingly effective tool for manipulation. And, apparently, it was a gift he had.

Her expression relaxed ever so slightly, causing a stab of guilt in his gut.

"You know, you're either nicer than I thought," she told him, "or more devious than I can understand."

"I'm much nicer than you think," Zach lied.

"Can you pick me up at home?"

He knew if he let her go home, she'd ditch the briefcase. That wasn't part of the plan. So, he made a show of glancing at his watch. "No time for that. We'll have to leave from here."

Her hesitation showed in the purse of her lips.

"I can pick you up at the bus stop again," he offered, knowing that would eliminate one of her hesitations.

It was her turn to glance at her watch. "Five minutes?"

He agreed. Then he watched until she got on the elevator. He wasn't going to risk her stowing the briefcase back in her office either.

At the opulent Boondocks restaurant, Kaitlin and Zach settled into a curved booth with Ray Lambert and his wife, Susan. The restaurant was on two levels, the upper overlooking the atrium that served as both an entrance and a lounge. Palm trees and exotic plants blooming from both floor and wall pots added to the fresh ambiance that included high ceilings, huge windows overlooking the park and natural wood and rattan screens to provide privacy between the tables.

Kaitlin had used the walk to the bus stop to call Lindsay and regain her equilibrium. Thank goodness some semblance of sanity had kept her from kissing Zach right there in the Harper building hallway.

She'd been inches, mere seconds, from throwing herself in his arms all over again and falling completely under his sensual spell. She was a fool, an undisciplined fool.

In desperation, she'd confessed to Lindsay and begged for a pep talk, needing to put some emotional armor around herself before the dinner started. As usual, Lindsay had shocked her back to reality, then used humor to put her on an even keel.

"Have we by any chance met in the past?" Ray asked Kaitlin as the two shook hands over a table set with silver, crystal and crisp white linen. Zach had slid partway around the booth seat and settled next to Susan, while Ray was directly across from Kaitlin.

"Once," she answered Ray. "Three years ago, at the NYAA conference. I was one of probably six hundred people who came through the receiving line."

He smiled at her. "That must have been it. I'm pretty good with faces."

Lindsay just hoped he wasn't remembering her ignominious firing from Hutton Quinn. Though, if he was, he didn't give anything away.

"Anyone else interested in the '97 Esme Cabernet?" Susan pointed to the wine list that was open in front of her.

Kaitlin was grateful for the change in topic.

"One of her favorites," Ray explained with a benevolent smile toward his wife. "You won't be disappointed."

Zach glanced to Kaitlin, obviously looking for her reaction.

She nodded agreeably, proud of the way her hormones were staying under control. This was a business dinner, nothing more. And it was going to stay that way. "I'd love to try it," she told Susan.

Susan smiled and closed the wine list.

A waiter immediately appeared beside their table.

While Ray ordered the wine, Kaitlin's attention caught on a couple crossing the foyer below. They were heading for the curved staircase, and even from this distance she could recognize Lindsay and Dylan.

She straightened to get a better view as they started up the stairs. What could they possibly be doing here?

Kaitlin couldn't miss Lindsay's red face. Her friend was furious.

"What the—" Though Kaitlin clamped her jaw on the unladylike exclamation, Zach swiveled to stare at her confusion. Then he followed the direction of her gaze.

Lindsay and Dylan had made it to the top of the stairs and bore down on the table. As they did, Zach sat bolt upright, obviously observing the fury on Lindsay's face.

The waiter left with the wine order just as Lindsay and Dylan arrived. They presented themselves, and Lindsay's quick gaze noted Ray and Susan. She schooled her features.

"I'm so sorry to interrupt." She smiled at Kaitlin, and her glance went meaningfully to the briefcase she held in her hand, moving it into clear view.

Burgundy.

It was Kaitlin's.

What was she doing with Kaitlin's briefcase?

"We just wanted to say hi," Lindsay continued, her voice full of forced cheer. "I met up with Dylan in the *garage*."

Kaitlin felt Zach stiffen beside her, while Dylan blushed.

Dylan? The garage? Her briefcase?

She felt her jaw drop open.

"We're going to get a table now," Lindsay announced smoothly, giving Kaitlin a soft squeeze on the shoulder. "Enjoy your dinner. But maybe we could talk later?" She hooked her arm into Dylan's and pasted him to her side.

Kaitlin couldn't help herself. She turned to gape at Zach in astonishment. Her briefcase had been in his trunk. How did Lindsay end up with it? And what was Dylan's connection?

Zach's face remained impassive as he focused beyond Kaitlin to Dylan. "We'll talk to you *later*."

Lindsay made a half turn to address Ray and Susan. "I'm really sorry to have interrupted. I hope you all enjoy your dinner."

Then she gave Kaitlin one ominous glance before propelling Dylan farther into the restaurant.

Kaitlin's immediate reaction was to follow them. But before she could rise from her seat, Zach's hand clamped down on her thigh, holding her firmly in place.

The action was shocking, the sensation electric.

"That was Dylan Gilby," he smoothly informed Ray and Susan. "Astral Air."

Kaitlin reached down to surreptitiously remove Zach's hand, but her strength was no match for his.

"I've met his father," Ray acknowledged. If he'd noticed anything strange in the conversation, he was too professional to let on.

"Dylan and I grew up together," Zach elaborated, filling the silence even while Kaitlin tried to work her leg free.

"Ah, here's the wine," Susan announced, looking pleased by the arrival of the steward.

As soon as Ray's and Susan's attention was distracted by the uncorking process, Zach leaned over. "Stay still," he hissed into Kaitlin's ear.

"What did you *do?*" Kaitlin demanded in an undertone.

"We'll talk later," he huffed.

"Bet on it."

"Stop struggling."

"Let go of me."

"Not until I'm sure you'll stay put."

"We first discovered this one in Marseille," said Ray, lifting his glass with a flourish for the ceremonial tasting.

Kaitlin quickly redirected her attention. She tried not to squirm against Zach's grip. His hand was dry and warm, slightly callused, definitely not painful, but absolutely impossible to ignore.

She wasn't wearing stockings today, and his hand was on her bare leg. His pinky finger had come to rest slightly north of her midthigh hemline. And his fingertips had curled into her sensitive inner thigh.

Now that her anger had settled to a hum, a new sensation pulsed its way through her system.

The touch of Zach's hand was turning her on.

Ray nodded his approval on the wine, and the steward filled the other three glasses before topping up Ray's.

When the wine was ready, Ray raised his glass for a toast. "A pleasure to meet you, Kaitlin. And congratulations on your contract with Harper Transportation. It's an important building."

"We're lucky to have her," Zach responded courteously.

Kaitlin thanked them both, clinked her glass against each of theirs, avoiding eye contact with Zach, then took a healthy swallow. The wine was incredibly delicious. More importantly, it contained a measure of alcohol to take the edge off her frustration.

Another waiter arrived with four large, leather-bound dinner menus, which he handed around to the table's occupants.

Zach accepted his with one hand, still not relinquishing his hold on Kaitlin.

She opened hers, trying to concentrate on the dishes and descriptions in front of her, but the neat script blurred on the page.

Had his hand moved?

Was it higher now?

Ever so slightly, and ever so slowly, but completely unmistakably his fingertips were brushing their way up the inside of her thigh.

Her muscles contracted in reaction. She could feel her skin heat, and her breathing deepened.

"The pumpkin soup to start?" he asked her, voice low and completely casual in her ear.

She opened her mouth, but she couldn't seem to form any words. She could barely sit still. Her toes curled and her fingers gripped tightly around the leather menu.

"Maybe the arugula salad?" he continued.

How could he do that? How could he sit there and behave as

if everything was normal, when she was practically jumping out of her skin?

"I'm going with the yellowfin tuna," Susan chirped.

Ray and Susan both looked to Kaitlin with questions on their faces.

Zach's hand slipped higher, and she very nearly moaned.

"Kaitlin?" he prompted.

She knew she should slap his hand away. She should call him right here, right now, on his unacceptable behavior. It would serve him right.

He'd be embarrassed in front of Ray Lambert. But then so would she. She'd be mortified if Ray—if *anyone*—knew what Zach was doing under the tablecloth.

"Arugula," she blurted out.

"The risotto is delicious," Susan offered helpfully.

Kaitlin tried to smile her thanks. But she wasn't sure if it quite came off, since she was gritting her teeth against Zach's sensual onslaught.

She balanced the heavy menu against the tabletop, holding it with one hand. Then she dropped the other to her lap, covering Zach's. "Stop," she hissed under her breath. "Please." The word came out on a desperate squeak.

His hand stilled. But then he turned it, meeting hers, and his thumb began a slow caress of her palm.

A new wave of desire flowed through her.

She could pull away anytime she wanted. But she didn't want to pull away. Lord help her, she wanted to savor the sensation, feel the raw energy pulse through her body. And when his hand turned back, and the caress resumed on her thigh, she didn't complain.

"The salmon," he said decisively, closing his menu and setting it aside.

Susan pulled her menu against her chest, speaking over the top. "The dill sauce is to die for."

Ray gave his wife's shoulder a quick, friendly caress. "It's beyond me why she doesn't weigh three hundred pounds."

"I have a great metabolism," Susan said, adding a self-deprecating laugh. "I don't do nearly enough exercise to deserve all those desserts."

Zach turned to Kaitlin, his fingertips still working magic as he spoke. "And what do you want?"

The double entendre boomed around them both.

Her gaze was drawn to the depths of his eyes, knowing there was no disguising her naked longing. "Risotto," she managed to say.

"And for dessert?" He pressed more firmly against her inner thigh, his palm sliding boldly against her sensitized skin.

"I'll decide later."

He gave a slow, satisfied smile, and a gleam of attraction turned his gray eyes to silver.

Just as she was tumbling completely and hopelessly under his spell, Lindsay's words came back to haunt her. *Do you think there's a slim possibility it was a distraction?*

Oh, no.

He was doing it, again.

And she was falling for it, willingly, and *all over again*.

Humiliation was like ice water to her hormones. She steeled her wayward desire, letting anger replace her lust.

"No dessert," she told him sternly, dropping her hand to her thigh and firmly removing his.

"Crème brûlée," said Susan. "Definitely crème brûlée for me."

Zach's gaze slid to Kaitlin for a split second. But then he obviously decided to give up. Distraction was not going to work for him this time. His behavior was reprehensible, and her lapse in judgment was thoroughly unprofessional. What would it take for her to learn?

Thankfully, Susan launched into a story about a recent business trip to Greece.

Kaitlin forced herself to listen, responding with what she hoped were friendly and intelligent answers to Ray's and Susan's questions, then asking about their trip to London and their new ski chalet in Banff, as appetizers, dinner and then dessert were served.

Zach didn't touch her again, luckily for him. Because by the time the crème brûlée was finished, the check arrived, and Ray and Susan said their good-nights, Kaitlin's mood had migrated to full-on rage.

As the waiter cleared the last of the dishes, smoothing the white linen tablecloth, Lindsay and Dylan appeared.

Lindsay plunked herself next to Zach, the briefcase between them, while Dylan sat much more reluctantly across from Kaitlin.

"They stole your briefcase," Lindsay said without preamble. "They *stole* your briefcase."

Kaitlin had presumed that was what happened. She immediately turned an accusing glare on Zach. There was no need to voice the question, so she waited silently for his explanation.

"It was in my trunk," he pointed out in his own defense. "*My* trunk."

Lindsay opened her mouth, but Dylan jumped in before she could speak. His blue eyes glittered at Zach. "Seems there are some finer points of the law you may not have taken into account here."

"They're *my* drawings," Zach stated.

The waiter reappeared, and conversation ceased. "May I offer anyone some coffee?"

"A shot of cognac in mine," said Lindsay.

"All around," Zach added gruffly, making a circle motion with his index finger.

Kaitlin wasn't inclined to argue.

"They are *my* drawings." Her words to Zach were stern as the man walked away.

"I paid you to make them," he countered.

"You *both* paid her to make them," Lindsay pointed out in an imperious tone.

"I wouldn't argue with her," Dylan muttered darkly.

Lindsay shot him a warning look.

He didn't seem the least bit intimidated by her professorial demeanor as he stared levelly back. "I had a math teacher like you once."

"Didn't seem to do you any good," she retorted.

"You stole my briefcase!" Kaitlin felt compelled to bring everyone back to the main point. "Was this entire dinner a ruse?"

She shook her head to clear it. "Of *course* it was a ruse. You're despicable, Zach. If I hadn't told Lindsay you'd invited me here. And if she didn't have a very suspicious nature—"

"A *correctly* suspicious nature," Lindsay pointed out to both men.

"—you'd have gotten away with it."

"I was planning to put it back," Dylan defended.

"I need to see the designs," said Zach, not a trace of apology in his tone. "My company, your company, pretend all you like, but I'm the guy signing the check. And I'm the guy left picking up the pieces once your game is over."

"That *game* happens to be my life." She wasn't playing around here. If she didn't fix her career, she didn't have a job. If she didn't have a job, there was nobody to pay rent, nobody to buy food.

He brought his hand down on the table. "And whatever's left when the dust clears happens to be mine."

Sick to death of the contest of wills, Kaitlin capitulated.

She waved a hand toward her briefcase. "Fine. Go ahead. There's nothing you can do to change them anyway. You don't like 'em, complain all you want. I will ignore you."

Zach wasted no time in snagging the briefcase from the bench seat between him and Lindsay. He snapped open the clasps, lifted the lid and extracted the folded plans. He awkwardly spread them out on the round table.

Just then, the waiter arrived and glanced around for a place to set the coffee.

Zach ignored him, and the man signaled for a folding tray stand.

Kaitlin accepted a coffee. She took her cup in her hand, sipping it while she sat back to wait for Zach's reaction.

She suspected he'd be angry. Her designs called for some

pretty fundamental and expensive changes to his building. But a small part of her couldn't help but hope he'd surprise her.

Maybe he had better taste than she thought. Maybe he'd recognize her genius. Maybe he'd—

"Are you out of your ever-lovin' mind?" His gray eyes all but glowed in anger.

Five

In the restaurant's parking garage, Lindsay twisted the key in the ignition of her silver Audi Coupe and pushed the shifter into Reverse. They peeled out of the narrow parking spot and into the driving lane.

"I suppose that could have been worse," Kaitlin admitted as they zipped toward the exit from the underground.

Zach had hated the renovation designs. No big surprise there. But since they were in a public place, he couldn't very well yell at her. So, that was a plus. And she wouldn't change them. He could gripe as much as he liked about a modern lobby not being in keeping with his corporate image, but they both knew it was about money.

Lindsay pressed a folded bill into the parking lot attendant's hand. "He *stole* your briefcase."

"I knew not seeing them was making him crazy," said Kaitlin, still getting over the shock at this turn of events. "But I sure didn't think he'd go that far."

Lindsay flipped on her signal, watching the traffic on the

busy street. "All that righteous indignation, the insistence on principles."

"I know," Kaitlin added rapidly in agreement. "The lectures, the protestations, and then wham." She smacked her hands together. "He steals the drawings right out from under my nose."

"I'm not a pirate," Lindsay mocked as she quickly took the corner, into a small space in traffic. "Nobody in my family was ever a pirate."

Kaitlin turned to stare at her friend. "What?"

"*We* have morals and principles."

"Are you talking about Zach?"

"Zach didn't steal your drawings."

"He sure did," said Kaitlin.

"Dylan was the guy with the briefcase in his hands."

"Only because Zach asked him to get it. Dylan's just being loyal."

"Ha!" Lindsay coughed out a laugh.

"Linds?" Kaitlin searched her friend's profile.

Lindsay changed lanes on the brightly lit street, setting up for a left turn. "What?"

"I say again. Do you think you're getting a little obsessed with Dylan Gilby?"

"The man's a thief and a reprobate."

"Maybe. But Zach's our problem."

Lindsay didn't answer. She adjusted her rearview mirror then changed the radio station.

"I think Zach'll leave it alone now," she said. "I mean, he's seen the drawings. He gave it his best—"

"You're changing the subject."

"Hmm?"

Kaitlin gaped at her friend in astonishment. All this fighting was a ruse. "You've got a thing for Dylan."

"I've got a thing for proving he's a pirate," Lindsay stated primly, sitting up straight in the driver's seat, flipping on the windshield wipers. "It's an intellectual exercise."

"Intellectual, my ass."

"It's a matter of principle. Plus, the semester just ended, and I'm a little bored."

Despite all the angst of the evening, Kaitlin couldn't help but laugh. "I think it's a matter of libido."

"He's incredibly annoying," said Lindsay.

"But he is kind of cute." Kaitlin rotated her neck, trying to relieve the stress.

"Maybe," Lindsay allowed, braking as a bus pulled onto the street. "In a squeaky-clean-veneer, bad-boy-underneath kind of way."

"Is that a bad kind of way?" The few times Kaitlin had met Dylan at the office, she'd mostly found him charming. He had a twinkle in his blue eyes, could make a joke of almost anything and, if it hadn't been her briefcase in question, she might have admired his loyalty to Zach for stealing it.

Lindsay gave a self-conscious grin, rubbing her palms briskly along the curve of the steering wheel. "Fine. You caught me. I confess."

Grinning at the irony, Kaitlin continued. "His best friend's locked in an epic struggle with your best friend. You've called into question the integrity of his entire family. And you practically arrested him for stealing my briefcase. But other than that, I can see the two of you really going somewhere with this."

Lindsay shook back her hair. "I'm only window-shopping. Besides, there's nothing wrong with a little libido mixed in with an intellectual exercise."

Kaitlin couldn't help laughing. It was a relief to let the anger go. "Zach groped me under the table during dinner. How's that for libido?"

Lindsay sobered, glancing swiftly at Kaitlin before returning her attention to the road. "Seriously?"

"I guess he's still trying to distract me."

They pulled into a parking spot in front of Kaitlin's apartment building, and Lindsay set the parking brake, shifting in her seat. "Tell me that's not why you showed him the plans."

"It wasn't *that* distracting." Well, in fact he was entirely *that* distracting. But the distraction was irrelevant to her decision. "I showed him the plans to shut him up."

"You're sure?"

"I'm sure." *Mostly.*

Lindsay gave a wry grin. "Poor Zach. Part of me can't wait to see what he tries next."

And part of Kaitlin couldn't help hoping it involved seduction.

In his office Monday morning, Zach was forced to struggle to keep from fantasizing about Kaitlin. He was angry with her over the lavish designs, and he needed to stay that way in order to keep his priorities straight. Thinking about her smooth legs, her lithe body and those sensuous, kissable lips was only asking for trouble. Well, more trouble. More trouble than he'd ever had in his life.

"—to the tune of ten million dollars," Esmond Carson was saying from one of the burgundy guest chairs across from Zach's office desk.

At the mention of the number, Zach's brain rocked back to attention. "What?" he asked bluntly.

Esmond flipped through the thick file folder on his lap. The gray-haired man was nearing sixty-five. He'd been a trusted lawyer and advisor of Zach's grandmother Sadie for over thirty years. "Rent, food, teacher salaries, transportation. All of the costs are overstated in the financial reports. The foundation has a huge stack of bills in arrears. The bank account has maxed out its overdraft. That's how the mess came to my attention."

Zach couldn't believe what he was hearing. How had things gotten so out of hand? "Who *did* this?"

"Near as we can tell, it was a man named Lawrence Wellington. He was the regional manager for the city. And he disappeared the day after Sadie passed away. My guess is that he knew the embezzlement would come to light as soon as you took over."

"He stole ten million dollars?"

"That's what it looks like."

"You've called the police?"

Esmond closed the file folder, his demeanor calm, expression impassive. "We could report it."

"Damn right we're reporting it." Zach's hand went to his desk phone. Someone had stolen from his grandmother. Worse, they'd stolen from his grandmother's charitable trust. Sadie was passionate about helping inner-city kids.

"We're having him arrested and charged," Zach finished, lifting the receiver and raising it to his ear.

"That might not be your best option."

Zach paused, hand over the telephone buttons. He lifted his brows in a silent question.

"It would generate a lot of publicity," said Esmond.

"And?" Who cared? It wasn't as if they had any obligation to protect the reputation of a criminal.

"It'll be a media circus. The charity, your grandmother's name, all potentially dragged through the mud. Donors will get nervous, revenue could drop, projects might be canceled. No one and no company wants their name linked with criminal behavior, no matter how noble the charity."

"You think it would go that way?" asked Zach, weighing the possibilities in his mind, realizing Esmond had a valid point.

"I know a good private investigative firm," said Esmond. "We'll look for the guy, of course. And if there's any benefit in pressing charges, we'll press them. But my guess is we won't find him. From the records I've reviewed, Lawrence Wellington was a very shrewd operator. He'll be long gone. Sadie's money's long gone."

Zach hissed out a swearword, dropping the receiver and sliding back in his tall chair.

The two men sat in silence, midmorning sunshine streaming in the big windows, muted office sounds coming through the door, the familiar hum of traffic on Liberty Street below.

"What would Sadie want?" Esmond mused quietly.

That one was easy. "Sadie would want us to help the kids." Zach's grandmother would want them to swiftly and quietly help the kids.

Esmond agreed. "Are you in a position to write a check? I can pull this out of the fire if you can cover the losses."

What a question.

Like every other transportation company in the world, Harper's cash flow had been brutalized these past few years. He had ships sitting idle in port, others in dry dock racking up huge repair bills, customers delaying payment because of their own downturns, creditors tightening terms, and Kaitlin out there designing the Taj Mahal instead of a functional office building.

"Sure," he told Esmond. "I'll write you a check."

He put Esmond in touch with his finance director, asked Amy to have Kaitlin come to his office, then swiveled his chair to stare out at the cityscape, hoping against hope his grandmother wasn't watching over him at this particular moment. In the three short months since her death, it felt as if the entire company was coming off the rails.

Not entirely his fault, of course. But the measure of a business manager wasn't how he performed when things were going well, it was how he performed under stress. And the biggest stress of his present world was on her way up to see him right now.

A few minutes later, he heard the door open and knew it had to be Kaitlin. Amy would have announced anyone else.

"You can close it behind you," he told her without turning.

"That's okay," she said, her footsteps crossing the carpet toward his desk.

He turned his chair, coming to his feet, in no mood to be ignored. He strode around the end of the big desk. "You can close the door behind you," he repeated with emphasis.

"Zach, we—"

He breezed past her and firmly closed it himself.

"I'd prefer you didn't do that." Her voice faded off as he turned and met her head-on.

She wore a slim, charcoal-gray skirt, topped with a white-and-gold silk blouse. The skirt accented her slender waist, and was short enough to show off her shapely legs, while the blouse clung softly to her firm breasts. The top buttons were undone, showing a hint of cleavage and framing her slender neck. A twisted gold necklace dangled between her breasts, while matching earrings swung from her small ears beneath a casual updo.

His gut tightened predictably at the sight of her, and he took the few steps back to the middle of the room.

Did she have to look like a goddess every day in the office? Had the woman never heard of business suits or, better yet, sweatpants? Could she not show up in loafers instead of three-inch, strappy heels that would haunt his dreams?

"I would prefer…" She started for the door.

He snagged her arm.

She glanced pointedly down to his grip. "Are you going to manhandle me again?"

Manhandling her did begin to describe what he wanted to do. He'd gone home Friday night with his muscles stretched taut as steel. He'd tossed and turned, prayed for anger, got arousal, and when he finally slept, there she was, sexy, beckoning, but always out of reach.

He searched her expression. "Am I frightening you?"

"No."

"I'm making you angry?"

"Yes."

"Deal with it." He wouldn't scare her, but he truly didn't care if she got mad.

She set her jaw. "I am."

"Because you're making me angry, too." That wasn't the only thing she was making him. But it was the only one he'd own up to—both out loud and inside his head.

"Poor baby," she cooed.

"You're taunting me?" *That* was what she wanted to do here? He could barely believe it.

"I'm keeping the upper hand," she corrected him, crossing her arms, accentuating her breasts, increasing his view of her cleavage.

He coughed out a laugh of surprise, covering up the surge of arousal. "You think you have the upper hand?"

"I *know* I have the upper hand. And there's nothing you can say or do to make me—"

He took a step forward. He was at the end of his rope here. The woman needed to wake up to reality.

Her eyes went wide, and her lips parted ever so slightly.

"Make you what?" he breathed.

"Zach." Her tone held a warning, even as her expression turned to confusion and vulnerability.

His attention locked in on her, and her alone.

"Make you what?" he persisted.

She didn't answer. But the tip of her tongue flicked out, moistening her lips.

He closed his throat on an involuntary groan, and his world shrank further.

He shifted closer, fixated on her lips.

His thigh brushed hers.

Her lips softened, and her breathing deepened.

He inhaled the exotic perfume, daring to lift his hand, stroking the back of his knuckles against her soft cheek.

She didn't stop him. Instead, her eyelids fluttered closed, and she leaned into his caress. His desire kicked into action. And he tipped his head, leaning in without conscious thought to press his lips against hers.

They were soft, pliable, hot and delicious. Sensation instantaneously exploded inside his brain. He was back on the yacht, the ocean breeze surrounding them, her taste overpowering his senses, the stars a backdrop to their midnight passion.

His arms went around her, and hers around him. Their bodies came flush, the sensation achingly familiar. She molded to him, fitting tight in all the right places.

He moved her backward, pressing her against the office wall. His hands slipped down, cupping her tight little bottom, resisting an urge to drag her sharply against his hardening body. He was on fire for her.

His hands went to her hair, stroking through the softness, cradling her gorgeous face while he peppered kisses, tracing a line over her tiny ear, down the curve of her neck, along her shoulders, to the edge of her soft silk blouse.

Her fingers twined in his hairline. Her lips parted farther, her tongue finding his, her perfect breasts pushing tightly against his chest, beading so that he could feel them. She stretched up, coming onto her toes, fusing her mouth with his, and slid her hands beneath his jacket.

Those small hands were hot through the cotton of his shirt. He wanted to rip it off, strip her bare, hold her naked body against his own and finish what they kept starting.

But a jangling phone penetrated his brain. Sounds from the outer office came back into focus. He heard Amy's voice. Someone answered, and he came to the abrupt realization of where they were.

He forced himself to stop, cradled Kaitlin's head against his shoulder, breathing deeply, all anger toward her having evaporated.

"We did it again," he breathed.

She stiffened, pulling away. "This is why I didn't want the door closed."

He let her go, pretending it wasn't the hardest thing he'd ever done. Then he forced a note of sarcasm into his voice, refusing to let her see just how badly she made him lose control. "You don't trust yourself?"

"I don't trust *you*," she told him for at least the third time.

Fair enough. He didn't trust himself, either.

But it wasn't all him. It definitely hadn't all been him.

She straightened her blouse and smoothed her hair. "What is it you needed to see me about?"

Zach forced himself to turn away. Looking at her was only asking for more trouble.

"Can we sit?" He gestured to two padded chairs at angles to each other in front of his floor-to-ceiling windows.

Without a word, she crossed to one of them and sat down, fixing her focus on a point on the skyline outside, folding her hands primly in front of her.

Zach's hormones were still raging, but he inhaled a couple

of bracing breaths, taking a seat and focusing his own attention on a seascape painting on the wall past Kaitlin's right ear.

"I just spoke to my grandmother's lawyer," he explained, composing and discarding a number of approaches on the fly. He had to convince her to pull back on the renovations. It was more important than ever, and he couldn't afford to screw this conversation up.

Kaitlin's attention moved to his face, her lips pursing, green eyes narrowing. "What do you mean by that?"

He gave up and met her gaze. She was so damn gorgeous, feisty, challenging. Even now, he wanted to take her back into his arms and change the mood between them. "Just what I said."

"What happened?" She jerked forward in her chair. "Am I out of the will? Did you find a loophole? Are you firing me?" Then she jumped to her feet. "If you're firing me, you should have said something before…" She gestured with a sweeping arm, across the office to the spot where they'd kissed. "Before…"

Zach stood with her. "I am *not* firing you. Now, will you sit back down."

She watched him warily. "Then what's this about?"

"Sit down, and I'll tell you." He gestured to her chair and waited.

She glared at him but finally sat.

He followed suit, refocusing. This wasn't going well. It was not going well at all. "A problem has come to light with my grandmother's charitable trust."

Kaitlin's features remained schooled and neutral.

"There's been some money—a lot of money—embezzled from the bank account by a former employee."

He paused to see if she'd react, but she waited in silence.

Zach leaned slightly forward, his feet braced apart on the carpet in front of him, choosing his words carefully. "Therefore, I am going to have to shift some cash from Harper Transportation to the trust fund, or some of her projects will collapse, like the after-school tutoring programs and hot lunches."

Kaitlin finally spoke. "Do you need me to sign something?"

Zach shook his head.

"Then what?"

"Harper Transportation's cash flow will be tight for the next year or so." He mentally braced himself. "So we may need to talk seriously about scaling back on the renovation—"

"Oh, no, you don't." She emphatically crossed her arms.

"Let me—"

"You mess with my emotions."

"I'm not messing with anything," he protested.

"Try to put me off balance," she accused.

"I'm offering you honesty and reason." He was. He was giving her the bald truth of the matter.

"One minute we're kissing—" she snapped her fingers in the air "—next, you're asking for concessions."

His anger trickled back. "The two were *not* related."

"Well, it won't work this time, Mr. Zachary Harper." She tossed her pretty hair, tone going to a scoff. "Embezzlement from dear ol' granny's charitable fund, my ass."

"You think I'm *lying?*"

"Yes."

What was the matter with her? He had documentation. It was the easiest thing in the world to prove.

"I'll show you the account statements," he offered. "The bank records."

"You can show me anything you want, Zach. Any high-school kid with a laptop and a printer in his basement can fake financial statements."

"You doubt the integrity of my accountants?"

"I doubt the integrity of *you.*" She came to her feet again, color high, chin raised, shoulders squared, looking entirely ready for battle.

Once again, he rose with her.

Though her hair was in an updo, she swiped her hands behind her ears, tugging at both gold earrings. "You've tried evasion, coercion, outright threats, theft, seduction and now emotional manipulation."

He clenched his jaw, biting back an angry retort.

"Good grief, Zach. Granny, a charity and hungry kids? I'm surprised you didn't add a dying puppy to the mix." She tapped her index finger against her chest. "I am renovating, and I am doing it my way. And for that, you get half a corporation and a divorce decree. It's a bargain, and you should quit trying to change the terms."

Zach fumed, but bit back his words. He knew that anything he said would make things worse. A contingency strategy was his only hope. And he was all out of frickin' contingency strategies.

Having apparently said her piece, Kaitlin squared her shoulders. She put her sculpted nose in the air and turned on her heel to leave.

As the door shut firmly behind her, Zach unclenched his fists. He closed his eyes for a long second. Then he dropped into his chair.

The woman was past impossible.

She was suspicious. She was determined. And she was oh, so sexy.

She was going to bring down a three-hundred-year-old dynasty, and he had no idea how to stop her.

"Plan C is a bust," he informed Dylan, spinning the near empty glass of single malt on the polished, corner table at McDougals.

Dylan dropped into the padded leather chair opposite, nodding to Zach's drink. "Well, at least you waited until five."

"I'm lucky I made it past noon." How could one woman be so frustrating? Her renovation plans went way beyond repairing her reputation. What she was planning to do to his building was just plain punitive.

Dylan signaled a waiter.

"I talked to a couple dozen more people today," said Zach. "Nothing's changed. I can get her an entry-level job, easy. But nothing that comes close to the opportunity she has at Harper Transportation."

The waiter quickly took Dylan's order and left.

Dylan shrugged in capitulation. "So, give it up. Let her go for it. You'll have a weird, incredibly expensive building. And you'll live with it."

"She's adding three stories," Zach reminded Dylan. "Knocking out nearly five floors for the lobby. Did you see the marble pillars? The saltwater fish tank?"

Dylan gave a shrug. "I thought they were a nice touch."

"I bailed out Sadie's charity today."

"Why?"

"Some jackass embezzled ten million dollars. My cash flow just tanked completely. So, tell me, Dylan, do I sell off a ship or slow down repairs?"

Dylan's expression and tone immediately turned serious. "You need a loan?"

"No." Zach gave a firm shake of his head. "More debt is not the answer."

"Another partner? You want to sell me some shares?"

"And be a minor partner in my own company? I don't think so. Anyway, I'm not mixing business with friendship." Zach appreciated the offer. But this problem was his to solve.

"Fair enough," Dylan agreed. "What are your options?"

"Nothing." Zach took a drink. He needed Kaitlin to scale back on the renovation. Short of that, his options were very limited.

Selling a ship was a stupid idea. So was slowing down repairs. He'd need the entire fleet up and running so they could capitalize on any rise in demand. A company the size of Harper Transportation had to have serious cash flow to keep going. More ships, more cash flow. Fewer ships would result in a downward spiral that could prove fatal.

"Always the optimist," said Dylan, accepting his own glass of Glenlivet from the waiter.

Zach tossed back a swallow. "Kaitlin is going to bankrupt me, and there's absolutely nothing I can do to stop her."

Dylan's voice went serious again. "What exactly do you need her to do?"

Zach spun the glass again. "Come to her senses."

"Zach. Seriously. Quit wallowing in self-pity."

Zach took a bracing breath. "Okay. Right. I need her to scale back. Build me a reasonable quality, standard office building. No marble pillars. No fountains. No palm trees. And no mahogany arch. And especially no two-thousand-gallon saltwater aquarium."

Dylan thought about it for a moment. "So, make her want to do just that."

"How?" Zach demanded. "I've tried everything from bribery to reason. It's like trying to use a rowboat to turn the *Queen Mary* around."

Dylan was quiet for a few more minutes. Zach tried to focus his thoughts. He tried to get past the emotions clouding his brain and think rationally. But it didn't seem to be working.

"What about Sadie?" asked Dylan.

"What about her?" Zach didn't follow.

"Sadie left Kaitlin the company."

"And?" How was that a plus in Zach's present circumstances?

"And Kaitlin would have to be downright callous not to care about what Sadie would want."

"You think I should convince Kaitlin to respect Sadie's wishes?" That would be an awful lot easier if Sadie had actually left wishes. But her only wish seemed to be for Zach's wife to control him.

Dylan lifted his glass in a toast, ice cube clinking against the crystal. "That's exactly what I think you should do."

"What wishes? Where wishes? Sadie left no wishes, Dylan."

"Would she want a flashy, avant-garde showpiece?"

"Of course not." Zach's grandmother Sadie was all about heritage and tradition. She had been the guardian of the Harper family history Zach's entire life, and she had an abiding respect for everyone that went before her.

"Then help Kaitlin learn that," Dylan suggested.

Zach couldn't see that happening. "She's already accused me of emotionally manipulating her."

"Did you?"

"No." Zach paused. "Well, I made a couple of passes at her. But it wasn't manipulation. It was plain old lust."

"Better stop doing that." Dylan drank.

"No kidding." Though, if Zach was realistic, it was probably a whole lot easier said than done.

Zach still couldn't see Dylan's plan working. "I doubt she'll listen to me long enough to learn about Sadie. And, even if she does, she'll assume I'm lying." At this point, there was no way Kaitlin would believe anything Zach said.

"Don't tell her about Sadie."

"Then how…" Zach tapped his index finger impatiently against the table.

Dylan gave a secretive little smile and polished off his drink. "Show her Sadie."

Zach gave his head a shake of incomprehension, holding his hands palms up.

"Take her to the island," said Dylan. "Show her Sadie's handiwork. Then ask her to design something for the office building that respects your grandmother. Kaitlin seems pretty smart. She'll get it."

Zach stilled. It wasn't a half-bad idea. In fact, it was a brilliant idea.

He let out a chopped laugh. "And you claim to be honest and principled."

"I'm not suggesting you lie to her."

"But you are frighteningly devious."

"Yeah," Dylan agreed. "And I've got your back."

Six

"He's after something," Kaitlin said as Lindsay plunked a large take-out pizza from Agapitos on Kaitlin's small, dining room table. "A guy doesn't make an offer like that for no reason."

Lindsay returned to the foyer, kicked off her shoes and dropped her purse, refastening her ponytail.

It was Sunday afternoon. The Mets game was starting on the sports channel, and both women were dressed in casual sweatpants, loose T-shirts and cozy socks.

"No argument from me," she said as she followed Kaitlin into the compact kitchen area of the apartment. "My point is only that you should say yes."

Kaitlin pulled open the door to her freezer and extracted a bag of ice cubes. "And play into his hands?"

Lindsay's voice turned dreamy. "A private island? Mansions? All that delicious pirate history? I don't care what he's up to, we're going to have one hell of a weekend."

Kaitlin paused, blender lid in her hand, and stared at Lindsay. "We?"

The announcer's voice called a long fly ball, and both

women turned to watch the television in the living room. The hit was caught deep in center field, and they both groaned their disappointment before turning back to the drink making.

Lindsay hopped up on one of the two wooden stools in front of the small breakfast bar, pushed aside the weekend newspaper and leaned on her elbows. "You're not going to Serenity Island without me."

"I'm not going to Serenity Island at all." Kaitlin dumped a dozen ice cubes into the blender. There was no way in the world she'd spend an entire weekend with Zach.

"It's the chance of a lifetime," Lindsay insisted.

"Only for those of us with a pirate fetish." Kaitlin added mango, pineapple, iced tea, mint and vodka to the ice cubes, mixing up their secret recipe for mango madness. It was a Sunday tradition, along with the take-out pizza and a baseball game.

"It's not a fetish," Lindsay informed her tartly. "It's more of an obsession."

Kaitlin hit the button on the blender, filling the apartment with the grinding noise. "You want to sleep with a pirate," she called above the din. "That's a fetish. Look it up."

Lindsay's grin was unrepentant. "First off, I have to prove he's a pirate."

With the mixture blended, Kaitlin hit the off switch and poured it into two tall glasses. Lindsay shifted back to her feet, headed for a cupboard and grabbed a couple of stoneware plates and put a slice of pizza on each of them.

"Here's something," Kaitlin began as they made their way back to the living room. "Put on that red-and-gold dress, and the Vishashi shoes, then tell him you'll sleep with him if he admits he's a pirate." She stepped to one side so that Lindsay could go around and take her usual spot on the couch beside the window.

"That's not ethical," said Lindsay with a note of censure.

Kaitlin scoffed out a laugh. "As opposed to arriving on his island to gather evidence against him?"

"It's not like I'm going to break into his house," Lindsay offered reasonably.

"You're definitely not going to break into his house, since we're *not going*."

"Spoilsport."

Kaitlin settled on the couch and snagged one of the plates of pizza, gaze resting on the baseball game while she took a bite of the hot pepperoni and gooey cheese. She sighed as the comfort food hit her psyche. "I don't want to think about it anymore."

"Going to Serenity Island?"

"Zach. The renovation. The arguments. The kisses. Everything. I'm tired. I just want to sit here, watch the game and dull my senses with fat and carbs."

"That seems like a big waste of time." But Lindsay took a bite of the Agapitos, extrathick, stuffed-crust pizza and stared at the action on the television screen in silence.

Though Kaitlin tried to concentrate on the players, her mind kept switching back to Zach and his possible motives for the invitation. "I wish I had your capacity for mental chess games," she ventured out loud.

"How exactly did he ask you?" asked Lindsay, shifting at her end of the couch so she was facing Kaitlin, obviously warming up for a good discussion.

Kaitlin thought back to the moment in her office. "He was polite—excruciatingly polite—and I think a little nervous. He said he wanted me to learn about his family, get a better understanding of his grandmother."

"Any kisses, caresses, groping…?"

Kaitlin made a gesture that threatened to toss her pizza at Lindsay. "Just words."

"Were you disappointed?"

"No."

"Are you lying?"

"Only a little." Zach was one incredibly sexy man and, for better or worse, he turned Kaitlin on like there was no tomorrow. She couldn't stop it. She could barely fight the urge to act on it. Which was why visiting Serenity Island was one very, very bad idea.

There was a full count on the batter, and they both turned to watch Campbell swing and miss.

Kaitlin took a generous gulp of the mango madness. Then she gestured with her glass. "I know he's trying to outsmart me."

"Good thing we're onto him," Lindsay said.

"He gets me alone, he'll try seducing me. I know he thinks it's to his advantage." And it probably was. She couldn't think straight when he kissed her. Heck, she couldn't think straight when he looked at her.

"So turn the tables on him."

"Huh?"

"Seduce him back."

Kaitlin nearly choked on her pizza. Seduce Zach? *Seduce* Zach? Why not just jump off the top of his building and be done with it? "Are you kidding me?"

"Two can play at that game, baby." Lindsay gave a sage nod. "Women have been getting their own way through sex for thousands of years."

"You want me to *sleep* with him?"

Zach was every woman's fantasy. He was rich, great-looking, smart and funny. He'd had women fawning over him since he was a teenager. He'd likely seen and done it all. It was laughable to think Kaitlin could hold her own in bed with Zach.

"He is your husband," Lindsay pointed out.

"He's not that kind of a husband."

"Okay. Forget that," said Lindsay. "But look at it this way. If we don't go to the island, he'll try something else. If we go, he thinks he's winning. But we're onto him, and we'll be waiting for his next move."

Kaitlin had to admit, Lindsay's logic had some merit. Trouble was, the thought of Zach's next move triggered a flare of desire that curled her toes.

They flew to Serenity Island in one of Dylan's Astral Air helicopters. It was the first time Kaitlin had flown anywhere. Vacations weren't part of her foster care upbringing, and airplane tickets were not something she considered one of the necessities of life.

Their first stop after landing on the island was Dylan's parents' house. It was adjacent to the private helipad. The Gilby garage was home to a small fleet of golf carts that Kaitlin and Lindsay were informed were the only motor vehicles on the island.

David and Darcie Gilby were away in Chicago on business, but their various housekeepers and caretakers were in residence, along with Dylan's aunt Ginny, who greeted the four of them in the foyer in a bright red, 1950s swing dress with a multistrand pearl necklace and clip-on earrings.

"Young people," she cried, taking both of Dylan's hands in her own. "So nice of you to bring company."

Ginny was a very attractive woman for what must have been her age. Her face was wrinkled, but her short white hair was perfectly styled with flip curls at the ends, and her makeup was flawless. Two little white puff-ball dogs trotted across the floor, nails clicking on the hardwood until they stopped beside her.

"Hello, Auntie," said Dylan, giving the woman a kiss on her powdered cheek. "How are you?"

"And which one of these lovely young ladies is yours?" asked Ginny, sizing up both Kaitlin and Lindsay, taking in their faces, hair and clothing as if they were in a pageant and she was the judge.

"We're just friends," said Dylan.

One of the dogs gave a sharp bark.

"Nonsense." Ginny winked at Kaitlin. "This young man's a catch." She moved closer, voice lowering as if she was confiding a secret. "He has money, you know."

Kaitlin couldn't help but grin.

"Now this one—" Ginny made a half turn and shook a wrinkled finger in Zach's direction "—he's always been a hoodlum."

"Hello, Aunt Ginny," said Zach, with what was obvious patience.

"Caught him in the linen closet with Patty Kostalnik."

"Ginny," Zach protested.

"Did you now?" Kaitlin asked the older woman, her inflection making her interest obvious.

"Or was it that Pansy girl?" Ginny screwed up her wrinkled face. "Never liked that one. She used to steal my crème de menthe. It was May, because the apple trees were blooming."

Kaitlin slid a glance to Zach, enjoying his embarrassment. He shook his head as if to deny the accusation.

"Kaitlin and Lindsay are staying at Zach's for a few days," Dylan told his aunt Ginny.

"Nonsense," Ginny retorted. "You need a wife, young man." She moved between Kaitlin and Lindsay and took each of them by an arm. "They need to stay here so you can woo them. Which one do you want?"

"They're staying with Zach," Dylan repeated.

Ginny clicked her tongue in admonishment. "You've got to learn to stand up for yourself. Don't let Zachary take them both." She looked to Kaitlin. "You want him?"

Kaitlin felt herself blush. "I'm afraid I'm already—"

She turned to Lindsay, her voice a bark of demand. "What about you?"

"Sure," said Lindsay with a mischievous grin. "Like you say, Dylan's a good catch."

Ginny beamed, while Zach chuckled, and a look of horror came over Dylan's face.

Ginny drew Lindsay off to one side. "Right this way to the kitchen, young lady. You can help me with the pie."

Dylan watched as they left the foyer and proceeded down a long hallway.

"You're not going with them?" asked Zach, still obviously controlling his laughter.

"She got herself into it," said Dylan with a fatalistic shake of his head. "The woman's on her own."

"That Pansy girl?" Kaitlin asked Zach, not ready to let him off the hook for that one.

"I was fifteen, and she was two years older."

"Uh-huh?" Kaitlin waited for more details.

"She taught me how to kiss," Zach admitted.

"And...?"

"And nothing. You jealous?"

Kaitlin frowned, sensing he was about to turn the tables. "Not me."

"Right this way," Dylan interrupted, pointing through an archway and ushering them from the foyer farther into house.

Kaitlin was happy to leave the conversation behind, and she was more than impressed by the house.

Only a few years old, the large and luxurious Gilby home was perched on a cliff overlooking the ocean and the distant coast of Connecticut. The west wall of the great room was two stories high and made completely of glass. Hardwood floors gleamed beneath open-beam ceilings, and a sweeping staircase curled toward a second-story overtop of the kitchen area where Lindsay had disappeared.

After Kaitlin had a chance to look around, they moved out onto a huge deck dotted with tables and comfortable furniture groupings. Large potted plants were placed around the perimeter, and a retractable roof was halfway shut, providing shade on half the deck and sunshine on the other.

"You must entertain a lot," Kaitlin said to Dylan, taking in the wet bar and two huge gas barbecues.

He nodded in answer to her question. "There's a great big party room downstairs. Plenty of extra bedrooms. And do you see those green roofs below the ridge?"

Kaitlin moved to the rail, leaning out to gaze along the steep side of a mountain. "I see them."

"Those are guest cottages. There's a service road that loops around the back. My mom loves to have guests here."

Kaitlin glanced straight down to see a kidney-shaped swimming pool with a couple of hot tubs beside it on a terra-cotta patio. The swimming area was surrounded by an emerald lawn. And, beyond the Gilbys' place, farther toward what looked like a sandy beach, and in the opposite direction of the cottages, she spied a stone spire and a jagged roofline that stuck up above the trees.

She pointed. "What's that down there?"

"That's Zach's place," Dylan replied.

Kaitlin glanced back at Zach in surprise. "You live in a castle?"

"It's made of stone," he replied, walking closer to the rail to join her. "And it's drafty and cavernous. I guess you could call it a castle. You know, if you wanted to sound pompous and have people laugh at you."

"It's a castle," she cooed, delighted at the thought of exploring it. "When was it built?"

"It's been around for a few generations," Zach offered without elaboration.

"Early 1700s," said Dylan. "The Harpers believe in honoring their roots."

Kaitlin's delight was replaced by an unexpected pang of jealousy deep in her chest. How many generations was that? Was there nothing not perfect about Zach's charmed life?

"I can't wait to see it," she said in what came out as a small voice.

Zach glanced sharply at her expression.

"The Harpers restore and preserve," Dylan explained. "The Gilbys prefer to bulldoze and start fresh."

"Philistines," Lindsay proclaimed as she breezed out onto the deck. In blue jeans and a green blouse, she somehow looked completely relaxed and at home.

Kaitlin, on the other hand, was now feeling awkward and jumpy. "How's the pie coming?" she asked, turning away from Zach's scrutiny.

Though she couldn't control her reflexive reactions, she had long since learned not to wallow in self-pity about her upbringing. It was what it was. She couldn't change it. She could only make the best of here and now. Well, maybe not exactly here and now. She only wanted to make it through the weekend.

"We're all invited, or should I say 'commanded' to stay for dinner," said Lindsay.

"That's Auntie," said Dylan, with a stern look for Lindsay. "You know she'll be fitting you for a wedding dress over dessert."

Lindsay fought with her unruly blond hair in the swirling wind, making a show of glancing around the deck and into the great room. "No problem," she informed him. "I could easily live here."

Dylan rolled his eyes at her irreverence.

"I've got nothing against living off the avails of pirating," she added with a jaunty waggle of her head. Then she tugged at the gold chain around her neck and pulled a gold medallion from below her blouse, swinging it in front of Dylan.

With a start, Kaitlin recognized it as the coin her friend had purchased from the antique shop. Lindsay was wearing it around her *neck?*

"What's that?" he demanded.

"Booty from your ancestor's plundering."

"It is not." But Dylan took a closer look.

"From the *Blue Glacier,*" she informed him in triumph.

"Okay. That's it." Dylan captured her arm and tugged her back across the deck. "Come here."

Kaitlin watched Dylan hustle Lindsay through the open doors into the great room. "Where's he taking her?" she asked Zach with curiosity.

"My guess is that he's showing her the Letters of Authority."

Kaitlin shook her head in amazement over their willingness to engage in this particular contest. "Lindsay spent two thousand dollars on that coin from the *Blue Glacier,*" Kaitlin told Zach. "Apparently, it was sunk by the *Black Fern* and Captain Caldwell Gilby."

"I know the story," said Zach.

"So, when do I get my ten bucks?"

He gave her a look of confusion.

"The bet at the baseball game," she reminded him. "Lindsay has unrefutable evidence that Dylan is descended from pirates. I believe that means she'll win the argument. And I believe that means you owe me ten dollars."

"Signed by King George..." Dylan's voice wafted through the open doors.

"Here we go," Zach muttered in a dire tone.

"It's still not legal," Lindsay retorted.

"Maybe not today."

Curiosity getting the better of her, Kaitlin settled to watch the debate through the open doorway.

Lindsay and Dylan were turned in profile. They were both obviously focused on something hanging on the wall.

"Forget the fact that Caldwell Gilby plundered in international waters," said Lindsay. "Just because a corrupt regime gives you permission to commit a crime—"

"One point to me," Kaitlin murmured to Zach.

"You're calling the British monarchy a corrupt regime?" Dylan demanded.

"That one's mine," said Zach, leaning back on the deck rail and crossing one ankle over the other.

"Your great, great, great, however many grandfathers held people at gunpoint—"

"Go, Lindsay," Kaitlin muttered, holding out her hand for the ten.

"I suspect it was swordpoint, maybe musketpoint," said Dylan.

"*Held* them at gunpoint," Lindsay stressed. "And took things that didn't belong to him."

Kaitlin gave Zach a smirk and tapped her index finger against her chest. Dylan didn't know who he was up against.

But Lindsay wasn't finished yet. "He sank their ships. He killed people. You don't need to be a lawyer to know he was a thief and a murderer."

"Oh, hand it over," Kaitlin demanded.

Dylan suddenly smacked Lindsay smartly on the rear.

She jumped. "Hey!"

"You crossed the line," he told her.

Kaitlin's jaw dropped. She sucked in a breath, waiting for Lindsay to react.

This was going to be bad.

Oh, it was going to be very, very bad.

Dylan said something else, but Kaitlin didn't hear the words.

In response, Lindsay leaned closer. It looked as if she was answering.

Kaitlin stayed still and waited. But the shouting didn't start, and the insults didn't fly.

Instead, Dylan reached out and stroked Lindsay's cheek. Then he butted his shoulder against hers and left it resting there.

For some reason, she didn't pull away.

Suddenly, Zach grasped Kaitlin's arm and turned her away.

"Huh?" was all she could manage to say.

"They don't need an audience," said Zach.

"But…" She couldn't help but glance once more over her shoulder. "I don't…" She turned back to stare at Zach. "Why didn't she kill him?"

"Because they're flirting, not fighting." Zach leaned on the rail, gazing into the setting sun. "Just like you and me."

The breath whooshed out of Kaitlin's chest. "We are not—"

"Oh, we so are."

"So far, so good?" asked Dylan, parking himself next to Zach at the rail of the deck after dinner. Lights shone from the windows of the Gilby house. The pool was illuminated in the yard below. And the twinkle of lights from Zach's house was visible in the distance.

"I think so." Zach motioned to the three women inside, where Ginny was playing right into his plan. "She's showing them photographs from when she and Sadie were girls."

"I dropped a hint to Lindsay," said Dylan, taking credit. "She immediately asked Ginny if there were any pictures."

"Good thought," Zach acknowledged. Ginny and Sadie had grown up together on Serenity Island. And though Ginny's short-term memory was spotty, she seemed to remember plenty of stories from decades back. She was in a perfect position to give Kaitlin some insight into his grandmother. And it had the added advantage of coming from a third party. Kaitlin couldn't accuse Zach of trying to manipulate her.

The thought that Zach could execute a master plan through the eccentric Aunt Ginny was laughable. Though, he supposed, that was exactly what they were doing.

"Lindsay's a fairly easy mark," Dylan added. "Mention a pirate, and off she goes like a heat-seeking missile."

"I notice you're protesting a bit too much about the pirates," Zach pointed out. Sure, Dylan was sensitive about his background, but Zach had never seen him pushed to anger over it.

"It sure makes her mad," Dylan mused.

"Our ancestors were not Boy Scouts," Zach felt compelled to restate.

"And the British monarchy was not a corrupt regime."

"There were a lot of beheadings."

Dylan shrugged. "Different time, different place."

"Yeah? Well, good luck getting Lindsay into bed with that argument."

Dylan's expression turned thoughtful. "Don't you worry about me. Lindsay likes a challenge. And I'm a challenge."

"That's your grand scheme?"

Dylan quirked his brows in self-confidence. "That's my grand scheme."

Zach had to admit, it was ingenious.

"Now let's talk about yours."

"Zachary?" came Ginny's imperious voice as she appeared in the doorway.

Zach glanced up.

"Over here," she commanded.

Dylan snickered as Zach pushed back to cross the deck.

Ginny beckoned him closer with a crooked finger.

"I need your help," she whispered, glancing into the great room.

"Sure." He bent his head to listen.

"We're going downstairs for some dancing." Ginny had always been a huge music fan, particularly of the big bands. And dancing had always been an important part of social functions on the island.

"No problem." He nodded.

"You ask the redhead, Miss Kaitlin." She gave Zach a conspiratorial nod. "I have a good feeling about the other one and Dylan."

"Lindsay," Zach prompted.

"He seems to have a particular interest in her rear end."

"Ginny."

She gave a short cackle. "I'm not naive."

"I never thought you were."

"You young people didn't invent premarital sex, you know."

Okay, Zach wasn't going anywhere near that conversation. "Dancing," he responded decisively and carried on into the house.

"Kaitlin," he called as he approached the two women huddled together on one of the sofas, their noses in one album and another dozen stacked on a table in front of them.

She glanced up.

"Downstairs," he instructed, pointing the way. "We're going to dance."

She blinked back at him in incomprehension.

He grinned at her surprise and strode closer, linking her arm and swooping her to her feet.

"Ginny's matchmaking," he whispered as they made their way to the wide, curved staircase. "I've been instructed to snag you as a partner so Dylan will ask Lindsay."

"She's very sweet," Kaitlin disclosed, sorting her feet out underneath herself.

"They're a family of plotters," said Zach.

"Yeah? Well, you're a fine one to talk."

Zach couldn't disagree.

They reached the bottom of the stairs, and the huge party room widened out in front of them.

"Wow," said Kaitlin, stepping across the polished, hardwood floor, moving between the pillars to gaze at the bank of glass doors that opened to the patio, the pool and the manicured lawn.

She tipped her head back to take in the high ceiling with its twinkling star lights. She put her arms out, twirled around and grinned like a six-year-old.

Not that she looked anything remotely like a child.

She wore sexy, high-heeled sandals and a pair of snug black pants. They were topped with a metallic thread tank that shimmered under the lights. While she moved, she reached up, raking her loose hair back with her fingers. It shone, and she shone, and he couldn't wait to hold her in his arms.

A member of the staff was working the sound system, and strains of "Stardust" came up to flow around them from a dozen speakers.

Ginny, Dylan and Lindsay arrived, laughing and joking as they spilled onto the polished floor.

"You need a partner, Auntie," Dylan declared, snagging her hand. It was obvious to Zach that Dylan knew exactly what his aunt was up to.

"Oh, don't you be silly," a blushing Ginny said, then slapped his hand away. "I'm far too old to dance."

Zach moved toward Kaitlin. She was definitely the one he'd be dancing with tonight. He took her easily into his arms, and moved them both to the music, swirling them away from the others.

"It's been a while since we did this," he murmured, as her body settled tentatively against his.

"And the last time didn't end so well," she pointed out. But she picked up the rhythm and ever so slowly relaxed into his lead as he stepped them toward the bank of windows.

"It could have ended better," he agreed. It could have ended with her in his bed. It should have ended that way.

He pulled back and glanced down at her beautiful face. Why hadn't it ended that way?

"Ginny said she was your grandmother's best friend when they were girls."

Zach nodded his concurrence. "Back then, my grandmother Sadie was the caretaker's daughter."

Kaitlin relaxed a little more. "Ginny said Sadie grew up here, married here and died here. All on this island."

Zach chuckled at the misleading description of Sadie's life. "They did let her off once in a while."

"Those are some really deep roots."

"I guess they are."

"Yours are even deeper."

"I suppose," he told her absently, more interested in paying attention to the way she molded against him than in talking about his family history.

She'd relaxed completely now. Her head was tucked against his shoulder, one arm around his back, their hands clasped and drawn inward, while her legs brushed his with every step.

As the song moved on, she eased closer. Their thighs met snugly together, her smooth belly and soft breasts plastered against him. Her heat seeped into his body, and he could smell the subtle scent of her perfume. It had to be her regular brand, because he remembered it from Vegas, from the yacht, from his office.

The song ended, but the sound of Count Basie immediately came up. "It Could Happen to You." Ginny obviously wasn't giving Dylan any opportunity to escape her planned romantic web with Lindsay.

Fine with Zach. Wild horses couldn't pull him away from Kaitlin.

"I was thinking—" he began.

"Shh," she interrupted.

"What?"

"Can you please not talk for a minute?"

"Sure?" But curiosity quickly got the better of him. "Why not?"

Her voice was low and sweet. "I'm pretending you're someone else."

"Ouch," he said gently, ignoring the sting of her words. Because she had pressed even closer, closing her eyes and giving herself up to his motion.

"I'm pretending I'm someone else, too." She sighed. "Just for a minute, Zach. Just for this song? I want to shut out the world and make believe I belong here."

His chest tightened.

He gathered her closer still and brushed a gentle kiss on the top of her head.

You do belong here, he silently thought.

Seven

Kaitlin had never in her life seen anything quite so magnificent as the Harper castle. And it truly was a castle. Made of weathered limestone, it had both chimneys and turrets. It was three full stories. And there looked to be what she could only imagine was an extensive attic network beneath the steep-pitched roofs.

Inside, wood panels gleamed, while ornate, suspended chandeliers bounced light into every nook and cranny. It was furnished throughout with antiques. Rich draperies hung from high valences and thick carpets muted footfalls and gave a welcoming warmth to the cavernous rooms.

Each of three wings had a showpiece staircase that wound up through the three stories and beyond. The biggest staircase began on the main floor in the entry rotunda. From the rotunda, Zach had shown them through the great hall, a beautiful library, plus drawing and dining rooms. The kitchen was fitted with modern appliances, but stayed true to its roots through wood and stonework and the gleaming array of antique copper pots and implements hanging from ceiling racks.

Last night, Kaitlin and Lindsay had each been appointed a

guest suite on the second floor. Zach's suite was on the third, while Sadie had converted the old servants' quarters to a private bedroom, bath and sitting room on the main floor. Zach told them that the bathrooms had been added in the early 1900s and updated every few decades since.

Five staff members lived in the castle year-round: a grounds-keeper, maintenance man, a cook and two personal maids to Sadie. Although the workload had obviously eased since Sadie's death, Kaitlin learned Zach kept them all on. They seemed very welcoming of company.

"Did you ever get lost in here?" Kaitlin asked Zach in the morning, as he showed her through a passageway that led to the north wing. Lindsay had left right after breakfast to swim in the pool at the Gilby house and, Kaitlin suspected, to flirt with Dylan.

"I must have as a little kid," he told her, pushing open the door that led to the pale blue sitting room that had belonged to Sadie. "But I don't ever remember being lost."

Kaitlin stepped inside the pretty room and gazed around with interest. "Can I get your cell phone number in case I have to call for help?"

"Sure," he answered easily from the doorway. "But you can orient yourself by the staircases. The carpets are blue in the main wing, burgundy in the north and gold in the east."

Sadie's sitting room housed a pale purple settee, several ornately carved tables and armchairs and a china cabinet with an amazing array of figurines, while a grand piano stood on a raised dais in the corner.

The morning sunshine streamed in through many narrow windows. Some were made of stained glass, and Kaitlin felt as if she should tiptoe through the hush.

She ran her fingers across the rich fabric coverings and the smooth wood surfaces, wandering toward the piano. "How old are these things?"

"I haven't a clue," said Zach.

She touched middle C, and the tone reverberated through the room.

"Sadie used to play," he told her. "Ginny still does some-times."

"I learned 'Ode to Joy' on the clarinet in high school." That about summed up Kaitlin's musical experience.

She made her way to a china cabinet, peering through the glass to see figurines of cats and horses and several dozen exquisitely painted teacups. "Do you think she'd mind me looking around like this?"

"She's the reason you're here," he replied.

Kaitlin suddenly realized Zach was still standing in the doorway. She turned in time to catch a strange expression on his face.

"Something wrong?" she asked, glancing behind her, suddenly self-conscious. Perhaps he didn't want her snooping through this room after all.

"Nothing." His response was definitely short.

"Zach?" She moved closer, confused.

He blinked a couple of times, drew a deep breath. Then he braced his hand on the door frame.

"What is it?" she asked.

"I haven't come in here." He paused. "Not since…"

Kaitlin's chest squeezed around her heart. "Since your grandmother died?"

He nodded in answer.

"We can leave." She moved briskly toward the door, feeling guilty for having done something that obviously upset him.

He shaped his lips in a smile and stepped decisively into the room, stopping her forward progress. "No. Sadie put my wife in her will. It's right that you should learn about her."

For the first time, it occurred to Kaitlin that in addition to being blindsided by the news of their Vegas marriage, Zach had likely been blindsided by the will itself.

"You didn't expect your wife to inherit, did you?" she asked, watching him closely.

He paused, gazing frankly into Kaitlin's eyes. "That would be an understatement."

"Was Sadie angry with you?"

"No."

"Are you sure?"

"I'm sure."

"Maybe you didn't visit her enough."

He shook his head and moved farther into the room.

Kaitlin pivoted to watch as he walked toward the windows. "Seriously. Would she have liked you to come home more often?"

"I'm sure she would have."

"Well, maybe that's—"

"She left you a few hundred million because I didn't show up here enough?" He turned back to face her, folding his arms over his chest.

Kaitlin took a step back, blinking in shock. "Dollars?"

"It wasn't like I never came home," Zach defended.

"Okay, I'm going to forget you said that." Kaitlin knew Harper International was a very big company, but hundreds of millions? All those zeros were going to make her hyperventilate.

"She did want me to get married," Zach admitted, half musing to himself.

But Kaitlin's mind was still on the hundreds of millions of dollars. It was a massive, overwhelming responsibility. How on earth did Zach handle it?

He swept his arm, gesturing around the room. "As you can probably tell, the Harper family history was important to Sadie."

"The responsibility would freak me out," Kaitlin confessed.

"The family history?"

"The millions, billions, whatever, corporation."

"I thought we were talking about my grandmother."

Right. Kaitlin pushed the company's value to the back of her mind. It was a moot point anyway. Her involvement would be short-lived.

"What did you do to make her mad?" she asked again, knowing there had to be more than he was letting on. Zach was right, Sadie wouldn't have cut him out of her will because he didn't visit often enough.

His lips thinned as he drew an exasperated sigh. "She wasn't mad."

Kaitlin crossed her arms over her own chest, cocking her head and peering dubiously up at him.

"Fine," he finally conceded. "She was impatient for me to have children. My best guess is that she was trying to speed things up by bribing potential wives."

"That would do it," said Kaitlin with conviction, admiring Sadie's moxie. She could only imagine the lineup that would have formed around the block if Zach had been single and word got out about the will.

"I'm not sure I want the kind of woman who's attracted by money," he stated.

"She was obviously trying," Kaitlin said, defending Sadie's actions. "It was *you* who wasn't cooperating."

He rolled his eyes heavenward.

"Seriously, Zach." Kaitlin couldn't help but tease him. "I think you should step up and give your grandmother her dying wish. Get married and have a new generation of little Harper pirates."

He didn't miss a beat. "Are you volunteering for the job?"

Nice try. But he wasn't putting her on the defensive.

She smoothly tucked her hair behind her ears and took a half step in his direction, bringing them less than a foot apart. "You want me to call your bluff?"

"Go ahead."

"Sure, Zach. I'm your wife, so let's have children."

He stepped in, bring them even closer. "And you claim you're not flirting."

"I'm not flirting," she denied.

"We're talking about sex." His deep voice hummed along her nervous system, messing with her concentration.

"We're talking about babies," she corrected.

"My mistake. I thought you were making a pass at me."

She inched farther forward, stretching up to face him. "If I make a pass at you, Zachary, you'll know it."

He leaned in. "This feels like a pass, Katie."

"You wish."

"I do." He didn't laugh. Didn't back off. Didn't even flinch.

They breathed in unison for a long minute. His gaze dropped to her mouth, and the urge to surrender became more powerful with each passing second.

He seemed to guess what she was thinking. "We won't stop this time," he warned.

She knew that.

If he kissed her, they'd tear off their clothes right here in Sadie's sitting room.

Sadie's sitting room.

Kaitlin cringed and drew away.

Zach's expression faltered, but she forced herself to ignore it, pretending to be absorbed in the furniture and the decorations, moving farther from him to peer through the door into Sadie's bedroom.

It took her a minute before she thought she could speak. "Sadie seems like she was an incredible person."

"She was," said Zach, his tone giving away nothing.

Maybe Kaitlin had imagined the power of the moment. "Do you miss her?"

"Every day." There was a vacant sound to his voice that made Kaitlin turn.

She caught his unguarded expression, and a lump formed in her throat.

For all his flaws, Zach had obviously loved his grandmother.

"Back then," Ginny informed Kaitlin and Lindsay from where she lay on a deck lounger, head propped up, beside the Gilbys' pool, "Sadie was a pistol."

While Lindsay was chuckling at Ginny's stories of growing up on Serenity Island, Kaitlin had been struggling to match the seemingly meticulous, traditional Sadie who'd been in charge of the Harper castle for so many years, with the lively young girl who'd apparently run wild with Ginny.

Both Kaitlin and Lindsay were swimming in the pool. Right now, their arms were folded over the painted edge, kicking to keep their balance while Ginny shared entertaining stories. The water was refreshing in the late afternoon heat. A breeze had come up off the ocean, and dozens of birds flitted in the surrounding trees and flower gardens.

Kaitlin was beginning to think Serenity Island was paradise.

"It wasn't like it is now," Ginny continued, gesturing widely with her half-full glass of iced tea. "None of these helicopters and the like. When you were on the island, you were here until the next supply ship."

"Did you like living here?" asked Lindsay, stretching out and scissor-kicking through the water.

"We constantly plotted ways to get off," said Ginny, with a conspiratorial chuckle. "Probably ten kids in all back then, what with the families and the staff. We were seventeen. Sadie convinced my daddy that I needed to learn French. *Mais oui.* Then I convinced him I couldn't possibly go to Paris without Sadie."

"You went to Paris?" Lindsay sighed, then pushed off the pool wall and floated backward in her magenta bikini. "I love Paris."

Kaitlin had never been to Paris. Truth was, she'd never left New York State. Shelter, food and education were the top of her priority list. Anything else would have to come after that. Though, someday, she'd like to see Europe, or maybe California, even Florida.

"We took one year of our high school in France," said Ginny, draining the glass of iced tea. "Came home very sophisticated, you know."

One of the staff members immediately arrived with another pitcher of iced tea, refilling Ginny's glass. She offered some to Kaitlin and Lindsay, filling up a fresh glass for each of them. They thanked the woman and set their glasses on the pool deck in easy reach.

Kaitlin had spent several hot hours today prowling through the castle. The dusty attic rooms were particularly hot and stuffy.

Now she was grateful for the cool water of the pool and the refreshing glass of iced tea.

Ginny waited until the young woman left the pool deck and exited back into the main house.

Then she sat up straighter, leaning toward Kaitlin and Lindsay. "Zachary's grandfather, Milton Harper, took one look at Sadie in those diaphanous Parisian dresses and, boom, she was pregnant."

Kaitlin tried to hide her surprise at learning such an intimate detail. Back in the 1950s, it must have caused quite a scandal.

Lindsay quickly returned to the pool edge next to Kaitlin. "They had to get married?" she asked.

Ginny pointed a finger at Lindsay. "I'm not recommending it to you," she cautioned. "You girls want to know how to catch a man nowadays?"

"Not necessar—"

Lindsay elbowed Kaitlin in the ribs. "How?"

"Withhold sex," Ginny told them with a sage nod. "They can get it any old place they want out there—" she waved a hand toward the ocean, apparently including the world in general in her statement "—but you say no, and he'll keep coming back, sniffing around."

"Auntie," came Dylan's warning voice. But it held more than a trace of humor as he strode across the deck in a pair of blue jeans and a plain T-shirt. "I don't think that's the advice I want you giving our lady guests."

Ginny harrumphed as he leaned down to give her a kiss on the cheek.

"You're cramping my style," he admonished her with good humor.

Ginny looked to Lindsay again, gesturing to her grandnephew. "This one's a catch."

"I'll try not to sleep with him," Lindsay promised. Then she covered her chuckle with a sip from her glass.

"You'll do more than try, young lady." Ginny, on the other hand, seemed completely serious. "I like you. Don't mess this up."

Lindsay sobered. "Yes, ma'am." But as she spoke, Kaitlin caught the smoldering look that passed between her and Dylan.

For all her plain-spoken, sage wisdom, Ginny had just made a fatal error with those two. She might as well have dared them to sleep together.

"Help me up, dear." Ginny reached for Dylan, and he grasped her hand, supporting her elbow, and gently brought her to her feet.

It took her a moment to get stabilized, and Dylan kept hold of her.

"Now that you're here," she said to him, "I thought I might call Sadie—" Then she stopped herself, a fleeting look of confusion entering her aging eyes. "Silly me. I meant the rose garden. I think I'd like to visit Sadie's rose garden."

Dylan slid a look of regret in Lindsay's direction. But there was no impatience in his voice when he spoke. "I'd be happy to drive you down," he told Ginny.

Kaitlin hopped out of the pool, adjusting her mint-green bikini bottom and making sure the straps had stayed in place. "I'll do it," she offered to both Ginny and Dylan.

She'd love to tour Sadie's rose garden. There was a picture of it in its heyday on the wall of one of the drawing rooms in the castle. She'd driven one of the little golf carts between the houses that afternoon, and it was very easy.

"Thank you, dear," said Ginny as Kaitlin scrubbed the towel over her wet hair. "You're a good girl. You should go ahead and sleep with Zachary."

Kaitlin stopped drying and blinked at the old woman in shock.

"Those Harper men aren't the marrying kind," Ginny elaborated.

"Zach already married Kaitlin," Lindsay offered. Then she froze halfway out of the pool. "I mean…"

"Are you pregnant?" asked Ginny, her gaze taking a critical look at Kaitlin's flat stomach.

Kaitlin quickly shook her head. "I'm not pregnant."

"I'm sorry," Lindsay squeaked in horror.

"Well, I don't know how you trapped him," said Ginny matter-of-factly. "Sadie and I have despaired that he'd even give any woman a second glance."

Kaitlin looked to Dylan for assistance. Did the situation require further explanation? Would Ginny forget the entire conversation by morning?

But he was too busy struggling to control his laughter to be of any help.

"We're, uh, not sure it's going to work out," Kaitlin explained, feeling as though she needed to say something.

"Well, how long have you been married?" asked Ginny, slipping a thin wrap over her shoulders, obviously oblivious to the undercurrents rippling through the conversation.

Kaitlin hesitated. "Um, a few months."

"Then you've already had sex," Ginny cackled with salacious delight.

"Who's had sex?" Zach's voice startled Kaitlin as he appeared from between two of the pool cabanas and came to join the group. His curious gaze darted from one person to another.

"You and Kaitlin," said Dylan.

"What?" He took in Kaitlin's bathing suit–clad body, his intense gaze making goose bumps rise on her skin and heating her to the core.

"Ginny and I are going to the rose garden," she announced, swiftly wrapping the big towel around her body. There was no reason she had to remain here. Dylan could bring Zach up to speed.

She and Ginny headed for the cabana that held her clothes.

Sadie's rose garden had obviously been a spectacular showpiece in its day. Some sections of the formal gardens had been kept up over the years by the castle staff, but it was obviously too much work to keep it all from overgrowing.

As Kaitlin and Ginny had made their way through the connected stone patios, beside gazebos, along stone trails and past the family's beautifully preserved chapel, Ginny shared stories of fabulous weekend-long garden parties, and of the dignitaries that had visited the island over the years.

Kaitlin got a picture of a carefree young Sadie growing into a serious, responsible young woman, with an abiding respect for the heritage of the family she'd married into. All signs pointed to Sadie and Milton being very much in love, despite the pregnancy and their hurried wedding.

Ginny clipped flowers as she talked, and Kaitlin ended up carrying a huge armful of the roses—yellow, white, red and pink. They were fragrant and gorgeous.

At the end of their walk, Ginny pleaded exhaustion and asked Kaitlin to take the roses up to the family cemetery and lay them on Sadie's grave.

Kaitlin had easily agreed. She'd delivered Ginny to the Gilby house and into the care of the staff there. Then she'd followed Ginny's directions and driven one of the golf carts up the hill to the family cemetery.

Visiting the graveyard was a surreal experience.

Isolated and windswept, it was perched on the highest point of the island, at the end of a rocky goat track that was almost more than the cart could navigate. She had stopped at the end of the trail to discover a small, rolling meadow dotted with Harper and Gilby headstones, and some that she guessed were for other island residents, maybe the ships' crews or staff dating all the way back to the pirates Lyndall and Caldwell.

Wandering her way through the tall, blowing grass, reading the inscriptions on the headstones, she could almost hear the voices of the past generations.

Both of the pirates had married, and they'd had several children between them. Kaitlin tried to imagine what it must have been like for Emma Cinder to marry Lyndall Harper in the 1700s. Did her family know he was a pirate when they agreed to let her marry him? Had he kidnapped her, snatched her away from a loving family? Did she love him, and was she happy here in what must have been an unbelievably isolated outpost? The castle wouldn't have existed, never mind the pool, the golf carts or the indoor plumbing.

While she read the dates on the old stones, Kaitlin couldn't help but picture Zach in pirate regalia, sword in his hand, treasure chest at his feet. Had Lyndall been anything like him—stubborn, loyal, protective? Had Emma fallen in love with Lyndall and followed him here? Perhaps against her family's wishes?

As she wandered from headstone to headstone, Kaitlin tried to piece together the family histories. Some of the lives were long, while some were tragically short. Clipped messages of love and loss were etched into each stone.

A mother and an infant had died on the same day in 1857. A tragic number of the children hadn't even made it to ten years old. There were few names other than Harper and Gilby, leading Kaitlin to speculate the daughters had married and moved off the island.

Most of the young women who'd married the Harper and Gilby men had given them children, then died as grandmothers and were buried here. In one case, Claudia Harper married Jonathan Gilby. But they didn't have any children. And that seemed as close as the families came to intermingling.

Then Kaitlin came to two new headstones—clean, polished, white marble set at the edge of the cemetery. They were Drake and Annabelle Harper. Both had died June 17, 1998. They could only be Zach's parents.

Though the roses were for Sadie, Kaitlin placed a white rose on each of Zach's parents' graves. Then she lowered herself onto the rough grass, gazing across the tombstones to the faraway ocean, trying to imagine how it would feel to belong in a place like this.

She turned her memory to the single picture of her mother, and to the sad rooming house where Yvette had ended up. Kaitlin drew up her knees, wrapping her arms around them, telling herself it was all going to be okay. She *would* nail the perfect renovation for the Harper building. Then she'd find herself a permanent job. She'd stay in New York, and Lindsay would be there with her.

She'd finally build herself a home, and things would be better than ever. Starting right now. She might not have roots. But she had prospects. She had ideas. And she wasn't afraid to work hard.

A raindrop splashed on her hand.

She blinked, raised her head and glanced over her shoulder to find that billowing, dark storm clouds had moved in behind her, changing the daylight to a kind of funny twilight.

She reluctantly came to her feet and dusted off the rear end of her shorts, smoothing her white blouse as droplets sprinkled on her hair and her clothes. With one last, longing look at the family cemetery, she made her way back to the electric golf cart at the head of the trail.

Her clothes damp now, she climbed onto the narrow, vinyl bench seat, pressed her foot down on the brake, turned the key to the on position and pushed on the gas pedal.

She pushed down harder, then harder still, but nothing happened. The cart didn't move forward like it should have.

She rechecked the key, turned it to off then back to on again. Then she went through the entire procedure a second time. Still, nothing happened. She didn't move.

Rain was coming down harder now, and the clouds had blocked the last vestige of the blue sky. The wind was picking up, whipping the fat raindrops sideways through the open cart.

Kaitlin whacked her palm against the steering wheel in frustration. The timing could not have been worse.

It might be a dead battery, or it might be a malfunction. Either way, she was well and truly stuck. She retrieved her cell phone, speed dialing Lindsay's number.

The call went immediately to voice mail.

Kaitlin left a message, hoping Lindsay wasn't holed up somewhere in Dylan's arms.

Okay, so she really didn't hope that. If Lindsay truly wanted to fulfill her pirate fantasy, then Kaitlin hoped that was exactly where she was. But she hoped it wasn't a long fantasy. And she truly wished she'd jotted down Zach's cell phone number when they'd joked about it this morning. She might not be lost in his castle, but she could certainly use his help.

She glanced around the wind- and rain-swept meadow, the tombstones jutting shadows in the gloom. She told herself there were still a couple of hours until dark, so there was plenty time for Lindsay to get her message. And how long could a person possibly frolic in bed with a pirate?

Okay. Bad question.

Thunder rumbled above Kaitlin, and a burst of wind gusted sideways, splattering the raindrops against her face.

Then again, maybe Ginny would wake up from her nap and tell them Kaitlin had gone to the cemetery. Assuming Ginny remembered that Kaitlin had gone to the cemetery. Would Ginny recall that?

Kaitlin peered once again at the tombstones on the horizon. She wasn't wild about sitting here in a graveyard in the middle of a thunderstorm. Not that she was afraid of ghosts. And if any of Zach's ancestors were ghosts, she had a feeling they'd be friendly. Still, there was a horror-movie aspect to the situation that made her jumpy.

The rain beat down harder, gusting in from all sides, and soaking everything inside the cart. Her shorts grew wet. Her bare legs became streaked with rivulets of water through the dust from the meadow. And her socks and running shoes were soaking up raindrops at an alarming rate.

She rubbed the goose bumps on her bare arms, wishing she'd put on something more than a sleeveless blouse. Too bad she hadn't tossed a sweater in the backseat.

Lightning flashed directly above her, and a clap of thunder rumbled ominously through the dark sky. It occurred to her that the golf cart was made of metal, and that she was sitting on the highest point on the island.

She wasn't exactly a Boy Scout, but she did know that that particular combination could be dangerous. Fine, she'd walk already.

There was still plenty of light to see the trail. It was all downhill, and it couldn't be more than forty-five minutes, an hour tops, to get back to Dylan's house.

* * *

"What do you mean, she's not here?" Zach studied a disheveled Dylan, then Lindsay. He didn't need to know what they'd been doing. Though it was completely obvious to anyone what they'd been doing. "Where would she be?" he demanded.

He'd checked the rose garden over an hour ago. He'd also combed through the entire castle, including the attic rooms and the staff quarters. And he'd just confirmed that Aunt Ginny was napping in her room. So the two of them weren't together.

"Maybe she went to the beach?" Lindsay ventured, ineffectually smoothing her messy hair.

"When was the last time you saw her?" asked Zach.

Dylan and Lindsay exchanged guilty looks.

"Never mind." What they'd been doing for the past three hours was none of his business. And they certainly weren't Kaitlin's babysitters.

"She can't be far," Dylan said. "We're on an island."

Zach agreed. There were only so many places she could be without having flown away on a chopper or taken a boat. And she didn't do either of those things.

There was the chance that she'd fallen off a cliff.

He instantly shut that thought down. Kaitlin wasn't foolish. He was sure she was fine. He watched the rain pounding against the dark window. It seemed unlikely she'd stay outside in this. So maybe she was already back at the castle. He could call—

Wait a minute.

"You've got her cell number," he said to Lindsay.

"Right." Lindsay reached for her pockets. Then she glanced around, looking puzzled.

After a few seconds, Dylan stepped in. "I'll check the pool house."

Zach shook his head in disgust. He did not want to know the details of their tryst. He pulled out his own phone. "Just tell me her number."

Lindsay rattled it off, and Zach programmed it into his phone then dialed.

It rang several times before Kaitlin came on the line. "Hello?"

Her voice was shaky, and the wind was obviously blowing across the mouthpiece.

She was still out in the storm.

"You okay?" he found himself shouting, telling himself not to worry.

"Zach?"

"Where are you?"

"Uh…"

"Kaitlin?" Not worrying was going to be a whole lot easier once he figured out what was going on.

"I think I'm about halfway down the cemetery trail," she said.

"You're *driving* in this?" What was the matter with her?

"Not driving, I'm walking."

"What?" He couldn't help the shock in his exclamation.

"I think the cart's battery died," she explained.

Okay. That made sense. "Are you okay?"

"Mostly. Yeah, I think so. I fell."

Zach immediately headed for the garage. "I'm on my way." Dylan and Lindsay came at his heels.

"Thanks," said Kaitlin, relief obvious in her voice.

"What were you doing up there?" he couldn't help but ask.

"Where is she?" Lindsay blustered, but Zach ignored the question, keeping his focus on Kaitlin.

"The roses," said Kaitlin, sounding breathless. "Ginny asked me to put the roses on Sadie's grave."

"Are you sure you're not hurt badly?" Adrenaline was humming through his system, heart rate automatically increasing as he moved into action.

The wind howled across the phone.

"Kaitlin?"

"I might be bleeding a little."

Zach's heart sank.

"I tripped," she continued. "I'm pretty wet, and it's dark. I can't exactly see, but my leg stings."

Zach hit the garage door button, while Dylan pulled the cover off a golf cart.

"I want you to stop walking," Zach instructed. "Wherever you are, stay put and wait for me. What can you see?"

"Trees." Was there a trace of laughter in her voice?

"How far do you think you've come?" He tried to zero in. "Is the trail rocky or dirt?"

"It's mud now."

"Good." That meant she was past the halfway point. "You want me to stay on the line with you?" he asked as he climbed onto the cart.

"I should save my battery."

"Makes sense. Give me ten minutes."

"I'll be right here."

Zach signed off and turned on the cart.

"Where is she?" Lindsay repeated.

"She was at the cemetery. Cart battery died. She's walking back."

Lindsay asked something else, but Zach was already pulling out of the garage, zipping past the helipad and turning up the mountain road. The mud was slick on the road, and the rain gusted in from all sides.

He knew he shouldn't worry. She was fine. She'd be wet and cold, but they could fix those problems in no time. But he'd feel a whole lot better once she was safe in his—

He stopped himself.

In his arms?

What the hell did that mean?

Safe *inside* was what he'd meant. Obviously. He wanted her warm and dry, just like he'd want any other human being inside and warm and dry on a night like this.

Still, it was a long ten minutes before his headlights found her.

She was soaked to the skin. Her legs were splattered in mud, her hair was dripping and her white blouse was plastered to her body.

As the cart came to a skidding stop, he could see she was shivering. He wished he'd thought to bring a blanket to wrap around her for the ride home.

Before he could jump out to help her, she climbed gingerly into the cart. So instead, he stripped off his shirt, draping it around her wet shoulders and tugging it closed at the front.

"Thanks," she breathed, settling on the seat next to him, wrapping her arms around her body.

He grabbed a flashlight from its holder behind the seat and shone it on her bare legs. "Where are you hurt?" He inspected methodically up and down.

She turned her ankle, and he saw a gash on the inside of her calf, blood mixing with the mud and rainwater.

"It doesn't look too bad," she ventured bravely.

But Zach's gut clenched at the sight, knowing it had to be painful. The sooner they got her home and cleaned up, the better.

He ditched the flashlight, turned the cart on and wrapped his arm around her shoulders, pulling her against his body in an attempt to warm her up.

"What happened?" he asked as they straightened onto the road, going back downhill.

"Ginny wanted to put the roses on Sadie's grave. But she was too tired after the tour of the garden." Kaitlin paused. "It's really nice up there at the cemetery."

"I guess." Though the last thing Zach cared about at the moment was the aesthetics of the cemetery.

Then again, Kaitlin was fine. She was cold, and she needed a bandage. But she was with him now, and she was fine. He reflexively squeezed her shoulders.

"I'm soaking your shirt," she told him.

"Don't worry about it."

"I feel stupid."

"You're not stupid. It was nice of you to help Aunt Ginny." It really was. It was very nice of her to traipse up to the cemetery to place the roses for Ginny.

"The other cart's still back there," she told him in a worried voice. "It wouldn't start. Did I do something wrong?"

"The battery life's not that long on these things."

She shivered. "Will it be hard to go and bring it back?"

"Not hard at all," he assured her. "But we'll wait until the rain stops before we do that."

The rain was pounding down harder now, the lightning strikes and thunder claps coming closer together. The cart bounced over ruts and rocks, the illumination from the headlights mostly absorbed by the pitch-dark.

"Thanks for rescuing me," she said.

Something tightened in Zach's chest, but he ignored the sensation. She was his guest. And there were real dangers on the island. The cliffs for instance. He was relieved that she was safe. It was perfectly natural.

"It was nothing," he told her.

"I was getting scared," she confessed.

"Of what?"

"I'm here on a mysterious pirate island, in a graveyard, in the dark, in a storm." Her tone went melodramatic. "The whole thing was starting to feel like a horror movie."

Zach couldn't help but smile at her joke. "In that case, I guess I did rescue you." He maneuvered around a tight curve, picking up her lightening mood. "And you probably owe me. Maybe you could be my slave for life?"

"Ha!" She knocked her head sideways against his shoulder, her teeth chattering around her words. "Nice try, Harper. First you'd command I stop blackmailing you. Then you'd make me divorce you. Then you'd fire me and kick me out of your life."

Zach didn't respond. That wasn't even close to what he'd had in mind.

Eight

In Kaitlin's guest bathroom, the claw-footed bathtub and
homemade lilac candles were completely nineteenth century.
While the limitless hot water and thick terry robe were pure
twenty-first.

She was finally warm again.

Zach had brought Kaitlin straight to her room in the castle,
where someone had laid out a tray of fruit and scones. He'd
called Dylan on the way to let them know everything was fine.
Half a scone and a few grapes were all she could manage before
climbing directly into the tub, while Zach had disappeared into
some other part of the castle.

Now the second floor was shrouded in silence. One of the
staff members had obviously been in her room while she bathed,
because the bed was turned down, her nightgown laid out and
the heavy, ornate drapes were drawn across the boxed windows.
She guessed they expected her to sleep, but Kaitlin was more
curious than tired.

On her initial tour of the castle, she'd discovered the family
portrait gallery that ran between the guest bedrooms and the

main staircase on the second floor. She'd glanced briefly this morning at the paintings hanging there. But now that she'd read the family tombstones, she couldn't wait to put faces to the names of Zach's ancestors.

She opened her bedroom door a crack, peeping into the high-ceilinged, rectangular room. There was no one around, so she retightened the belt on the thick, white robe and tiptoed barefoot over the richly patterned carpet.

Chandeliers shone brightly, suspended from the arched, stone ceiling at intervals along the gallery. Smaller lights illuminated individual paintings, beginning with Lyndall Harper himself at one end. He looked maybe forty-five, a jeweled sword hilt in his hand, blade pointing to the floor. She couldn't help but wonder how many battles the sword had seen. Had he used it to vanquish enemies, maybe kill innocent people before stealing their treasure and taking their ships?

Of course he had.

He was a pirate.

She returned her attention to his face, shocked when she realized how much he looked like Zach. A few years older, a few pounds heavier, and there were a few more scars to his name. But the family resemblance was strong, eerily strong.

She left the painting and moved along the wall, counting down the generations to the portrait of Zach's father at the opposite end. She guessed Zach had yet to be immortalized. Maybe he'd refused to sit still long enough for his image to be painted.

She smiled at the thought.

She'd counted twelve generations between Lyndall and Zach. The paintings on this wall were all men. But she'd noticed the ladies' portraits were hung on the opposite side of the room.

She walked her way back, studying Lyndall all over again. The main staircase of the grand hall was behind him in the painting, so he'd definitely been the one to build the castle. It was strange to stand on a spot in a room, then see that same place depicted nearly three hundred years earlier. She shivered at the notion of the pirate Lyndall walking this same floor.

"Scary, isn't it?" came Zach's voice, his footfalls muted against the carpet.

For some reason, his voice didn't startle her.

"He looks just like you." She twisted, squinting from one man to the other.

"Want to see something even stranger?" He cocked his head and moved toward the wall of ladies' portraits.

Kaitlin followed him across the room.

"Emma Cinder." He nodded to the painting. "She was Lyndall's wife."

The woman sat prim and straight at a scarred wooden table, her long red hair twisted into a crown of braids. She was sewing a sampler, wearing green robes over a thin, champagne-colored, low-cut blouse with a lace fringe that barely covered her nipples. Her red lips were pursed above a delicate chin. Her cheeks were flushed. And her deep green eyes were surrounded by thick, dark lashes.

"Wow," said Kaitlin. "You don't think ten-times great-grandma when you see her."

Zach chuckled. "Look closer."

Kaitlin squinted. "What am I looking for?"

"The auburn hair, the green eyes, those full, bow-shaped lips, the curve of her chin."

Kaitlin glanced up at him in confusion.

He smoothed his hand over her damp hair. "She looks a lot like you."

"She does not." But Kaitlin's gaze moved back to the painting, peering closer.

"She sure does."

"Okay, maybe a little bit," she admitted. Their eyes were approximately the same shape, and the hair color was the same. But there were probably thousands of women in New York with green eyes and long, auburn hair.

"Maybe a lot," said Zach.

"Where was she from?" Kaitlin's curiosity was even stronger now than it had been in the cemetery. What could have brought Emma to Serenity Island with Lyndall?

"She was from London," said Zach. "A seamstress I was told. The daughter of a tavern owner."

"And she married a pirate?" Kaitlin had to admit, Lyndall was a pretty good-looking pirate. But still...

"He kidnapped her."

"No way."

Zach leaned down to Kaitlin's ear, lowering his voice to an ominous tone. "Tossed her on board his ship and, I'm assuming, had his way with her all the way across the Atlantic."

Kaitlin itched to reach up and touch the portrait. "And then they got married?"

"Then they got married."

"Do you think she was happy here? With him?" For some reason, it was important to Kaitlin to believe Emma had been happy.

"It's hard to say. I've read a few letters that she got from her family back in England. They're chatty, newsy, but they're not offering to come rescue her. So I guess she must have been okay."

"Poor thing," said Kaitlin.

"He built her a castle. And they had four children. Look here." Zach gently grasped Kaitlin's shoulders and turned her to guide her back to the men's portrait wall.

She liked it that he was touching her. There was something comforting about his broad hands firmly holding her shoulders. He'd kept his arm around her the whole ride back from the cemetery, his body offering what warmth he could in the whipping wind. And that had been comforting, too.

"Their eldest son, Nelson," said Zach, gesturing to the portrait with one hand, leaving the other gently resting on her shoulder.

"What about the rest of the children?"

"Sadie has their portraits scattered in different rooms. The other two sons died while they were still children, and the daughter went back to a convent in London."

"I saw the boys' tombstones," said Kaitlin. "Harold and William?"

"Good memory." Zach brushed her damp hair back from her face, and for some reason, she was suddenly reminded of what she was wearing.

She was naked under the white robe, her skin glowing warm, getting warmer by the minute. She realized the lapels had gaped open, and she realized the opening had Zach's attention.

Their silence charged itself with electricity.

She knew she should pull the robe closed again, but her hands stayed fast by her sides.

Zach made a half turn toward her.

His hand slowly moved from her shoulder to her neck, his fingertips brushing against her sensitive skin.

"Sometimes I think they had it easy." Zach's voice was a deep, powerful hum.

"Who?" she managed to breathe. Every fiber of her attention was on the insubstantial brush of his hand.

His other hand came up to close on the lapel of her robe. "The pirates," he answered. "They ravage first, and ask questions later."

He tugged on the robe, pulling her to him, and his mouth came down on hers. It was hot, firm, open and determined.

She swayed from the intense sensation, but his arm went around her waist to hold her steady as the kiss went on and on.

He tugged the sash of the robe, releasing the knot, so it fell open. His free hand slipped inside, encircling her waist again, pulling her bare breasts against the texture of his shirt.

Her arms were lost in the big sleeves, too tangled to be of any use. But she breathed his name, parted her lips, welcomed his tongue into the depths of her mouth.

His wide hand braced her rib cage, thumb brushing the tender skin beneath her breast. Her nipples peaked, a tingle rushing to their delicate skin. Her thighs relaxed, reflexively easing apart, and he moved between them, the denim of his pants sending shock waves through her body.

He deftly avoided the portrait as he pressed her against the smooth stone of the wall. His hand cupped her breast. His lips found her ear, her neck, the tip of her shoulder, as he pushed the robe off. It pooled at her feet, and she was completely naked.

He drew back for a split second, gazing down, drinking in the picture of her body.

"Gorgeous," he breathed, lips back to hers, hands stroking her spine, down over her buttocks, to the back of her thighs. Then up over her hips, her belly, her breasts. She gasped as he stroked his fingertips across her nipples, the sensation near painful, yet exquisite.

His hands traced her arms, twining his fingers with hers, then holding them up, braced against the wall while his mouth made its moves on her body. He pressed hot, openmouthed kisses from her lips to her neck, found her breasts, drawing each nipple into the heat, suckling until she thought her legs would give way beneath her.

She groaned his name in a plea.

He was back to her mouth, his hands moving down, covering her breasts, taking over from his lips, thumbs stroking across her wet nipples.

She tangled her hands in his hair, pushing his mouth harder against hers, kissing deeper, mind blank to everything but his taste and touch. One of his hands moved lower, stroking over her belly, toying with her silky hair, sliding forward.

She wrapped her arms around him, anchoring her body more tightly against him, saving her failing legs, burying her face in the crook of his neck and tonguing the salt taste from his skin.

His fingers slipped inside her, and a lightning bolt electrified her brain. She cried out his name, an urgency blinding her. She fumbled with the button on his jeans, dragging down the zipper.

He cupped her bottom, lifting her, spreading her legs, bracing her against the cool wall.

A small semblance of sanity remained.

"Protection?" she gasped.

"Got it."

One arm braced her bottom, while his hand cupped her chin.

He kissed her deeply, their bodies pressed together, her nerves screaming almost unbearably for completion.

"Now," she moaned. "Please, now."

It took him a second, and then he was inside her, his heat sliding home in a satisfying rush that made her bones turn to liquid and the air whoosh out of her lungs.

Her hands fisted and her toes curled as she surrendered herself to the rhythm of his urgent lovemaking. Her head tipped back, the high ceiling spinning above her. Lightning lit up the high windows, while thunder vibrated the stone walls of the castle.

She arched against him, struggling to get closer. Her breaths came in gasps, while the pulsating buzz that started at her center radiated out to overwhelm her entire body.

She cried his name again, and he answered with a guttural groan. Then the storm, the castle and their bodies throbbed together as one.

When the universe righted itself, Kaitlin slowly realized what they'd just done.

Bad enough that they'd made love with each other. But they weren't locked up in some safe, private bedroom. She was naked, in an open room of the castle, where five other people worked and lived. Any one of them could have walked up the staircase at any moment.

She let out a pained groan.

"You okay?" Zach gasped, glancing between them and around them.

"Somebody could have seen us," she whispered.

He tightened his hold on her. "Nobody would do that."

"Not on *purpose*."

"The staff are very discreet."

"Well, apparently we're not."

"God, you feel good."

She couldn't help stealing another glance toward the staircase. "I'm completely naked."

He chuckled low. "We just gave in, broke all our promises, consummated our marriage, and you're worried because somebody *might* have seen us?"

"Yes," she admitted in a small voice. She hadn't really had time to think about the consummation angle. More that they had, foolishly, given in to their physical attraction.

"You're delightful," he told her.

"That sounded patronizing."

"Did it?" His voice dropped to a sensual hush, and his mouth moved in on hers. "Because patronizing is the last thing I'm feeling right now."

His kiss was long and deep and thorough. And by the time he drew back, the pulse of arousal was starting all over in her body. She wanted him. Still.

"Again?" he asked, nibbling at her ear, his palm sliding up her rib cage toward her breast.

"Not here." She didn't want to risk it again.

"Okay by me." He gently eased himself from her body, flicked the button to close his pants, then lifted her solidly into the cradle of his arms and headed for the staircase to his bedroom.

"My robe," she protested.

"You won't need it."

Zach held Kaitlin naked in his arms, inhaling the coconut scent of her hair, reveling in the silk of her smooth skin beneath his fingertips. A sheet half covered them, but his quilts had long since been shoved off the king-size bed.

"This is gorgeous," she breathed, one hand wrapped around the ornately carved bedpost, as she gazed up at the scrollwork on his high ceiling.

"*This* is gorgeous," he corrected, stroking his way across her smooth belly to the curve of her hip bone.

She looked great in his bed, her shimmering, auburn hair splayed across his pillowcase, her ivory skin glowing against his gold silk sheets.

"I never knew people lived like this." She captured his hand that had wandered to her thigh, giving his palm a lingering kiss.

"It took me a while to figure out some people didn't," he admitted.

She released his hand and came up on one elbow. "Were you by any chance a spoiled child?"

"I wouldn't call it spoiled." He couldn't stop touching her, so he ran his palm over the curve of her hip, tracing down her shapely thigh to the tender skin behind her knee. "But I was about five before I realized everybody didn't have their own castle."

Kaitlin's eyes clouded, and she went silent.

He wanted to prompt her, but he forced himself to stay silent.

She finally spoke in a small voice. "I was about five when I realized most people had parents."

Her words shocked him to the core, and his hand stilled in its exploration. "You grew up without parents?"

She nodded, rolling to her back, a slow blink camouflaging the emotion in her eyes.

"What happened?" he asked, watching her closely.

"My mom died when I was born. She had no relatives that I ever found."

"Katie," he breathed, not knowing what else to say, his heart instantly going out to her.

She'd never mentioned her family. So he'd assumed they weren't close. He thought maybe they lived in another part of the country, Chicago perhaps, or maybe California.

"She either didn't know, or didn't say who my father was." Kaitlin made a square shape in the air with both hands. "Unknown. That's what it says on my birth certificate. Father—unknown."

Zach's hand clenched convulsively where it rested on her hip.

"I never knew," he said. Though he realized the statement was meaningless. Of course he never knew. Then again, he'd never asked. Because he hadn't wanted to know anything about her personal life. He simply wanted to finish off their business and have her gone.

Now, he felt like a heel.

"I used to wonder who she was," Kaitlin mused softly, half to herself. "A runaway princess. An orphan. Maybe a prostitute." Then her voice grew stronger, a trace of wry humor in its depths.

"Perhaps I'm descended from a hooker and her customer. What do you suppose that means?"

Zach brushed a lock of her hair back from her forehead. "I think it means you have a vivid imagination."

"It could be true," Kaitlin insisted.

"I suppose." Since the idea didn't seem to upset her, his fingertips went back to tracing a pattern on her stomach. "I guess I'm the rouge pirate, and you're the soiled dove." He brushed his knuckles against the skin beneath her bare breast. "Just so you know. That's working for me."

She lifted a pillow and halfheartedly thwacked him in the side of the head. "Everything seems to work for you."

"Only when it comes to you." He tossed the pillow out of the way, acknowledging the words were completely true. He leaned up and gently stroked her face. "Were you adopted?"

She was silent for a long moment, while her clouded jade eyes put a hundred lonely images into his brain. He regretted the question, but he couldn't call it back.

"Foster homes," she finally told him.

The simple words made his chest thump with regret. He thought back to all the heirlooms he'd shown her. The family history. The portraits, the cemetery.

"I'm so sorry," he told her. "I can't believe I threw my castle up in your face."

"You didn't know," she repeated.

"I wish I had."

"Well, *I* wish I'd grown up in a castle." Her spunk was back, and the strength of character surprised and impressed him. "But that's the way it goes," she concluded.

"We had extra rooms and everything," he teased in an attempt to keep things light.

"Could you not have come and found me sooner?"

He sobered, completely serious. "I wish I had."

Her grin slowly faded, but not to sadness.

His own want growing, he shifted forward and kissed her lips, drawing her tenderly but fully into his arms again, feeling aroused and protective all at the same time. "Was it awful?" he had to risk asking.

"It was lonely," she whispered into the crook of his neck. Then she coughed out a laugh and arched away. "I can't believe I'm telling this to you...*you* of all people."

"What about me?" He couldn't help feeling vaguely hurt.

"You're the guy who's ruining my life."

"Huh?"

She glanced around his room and spread her arms wide. "What the hell have we done?"

"We're married," he responded.

"By *Elvis*." She suddenly clambered out of bed.

He didn't want her to go, couldn't let her go.

"My robe?" she asked.

"Downstairs."

She swore.

"You don't have to leave," he pointed out. She could stay here, sleep here, lay here in his arms all night long.

She turned to face him, still naked, still glorious, still the most amazing person he'd ever met.

"This was a mistake," she told him in no uncertain terms.

He climbed out the opposite side of the bed to face her. "It may have made things a little more complicated," he conceded.

"A *little* more complicated?"

"Nothing needs to change."

"Everything just changed." She spotted his shirt, discarded on the floor, and scooped it up. "We never should have given into chemistry, Zach. Just so you know, this doesn't mean you have an advantage over me."

"What?" He wasn't following her logic.

"I have to call Lindsay." She glanced around the room. "She's probably downstairs. She's probably wondering where the heck I've gone."

"Lindsay's not downstairs," Zach announced with certainty.

Kaitlin pulled his big shirt over her head. "How would you know that?"

Zach made his way around the foot of the bed. "Lindsay's not coming back here tonight."

"But—" Kaitlin stilled. After a second, she seemed to correctly interpret the meaningful look in his eyes. "Really?"

"Really."

"You sure they did?"

"Oh, I'm sure." Zach had known Dylan his entire life. He'd seen the way Dylan looked at Lindsay. He'd also seen the way Lindsay looked back.

Kaitlin still seemed skeptical. "She said she wouldn't sleep with him until he admitted he was a pirate."

Zach barked out a laugh at an absurd memory. "I guess that explains it."

"Explains what?"

"The Jolly Roger flying over the pool house."

Kaitlin fought a grin and lost. "I want my ten bucks."

He moved closer, desperate to take her back into his arms. "Katie, you can have anything you want."

She gazed up at him. "I want to renovate your building. My way." Then she paused, tilting her head. "This has been a recorded message."

"I guess adding the condition that you sleep with me to seal the deal would be inappropriate?"

"And illegal."

"I'm a pirate, what the hell do I care about legal?"

She didn't answer him, but she didn't move away, either.

He curled his hands into fists to keep from touching her. "Sleep with me, Katie."

She hesitated, and he held his breath.

Her gaze darted in all directions, while her teeth trapped her bottom lip.

He was afraid to push, afraid not to.

Finally, he tossed caution to the wind, reaching out, snagging a handful of his shirt, drawing her to him and wrapping her deep in his arms. "I can't let you go yet."

Maybe tomorrow. Maybe never.

* * *

"It was the best pie I have *ever* tasted," Lindsay said to Kaitlin, her voice bubbling through the Gilby kitchen while Ginny scooped flour into a big steel bowl.

"My grandmother taught me that recipe," said Ginny, wiping her hands on a voluminous white apron that covered her red-and-white polka-dot dress. She had red-heeled pumps to match, and a spray of lace and plastic cherries was pinned into her hair as a small hat.

Kaitlin was fairly certain Ginny thought it was 1952.

"It's the chill on the lard, you know," Ginny continued her instructions, seeming to be in her element with the two younger women as baking students. "You need the temperature, the cutting, the mixing. Half in first. Like this."

"Do you refrigerate it?" asked Kaitlin, glancing from the stained recipe card to the bowl, watching Ginny's hands closely as they mixed the ingredients. She and Lindsay had been given the task of cutting and peeling apples and floating them in a bowl of cold water.

Ginny giggled. "That's the secret, girls." She lowered her voice, glancing around as if to make sure they were alone in the big Gilby kitchen. "We keep it in the wine cellar."

Lindsay grinned at Kaitlin, and Kaitlin grinned right back, thoroughly enjoying herself. Nobody had ever taught her to bake before. She'd watched a few cooking shows, and sometimes made cupcakes from a mix, but mostly she bought Sugar Bob's and she sure never had a sweet old lady walk her through a traditional family recipe.

"Best way to trap a man," said Ginny. "Feed him a good pie."

"Were you ever married?" asked Kaitlin. Ginny used the Gilby last name, but that might not mean anything. And she certainly seemed obsessed with getting men.

"Me?" Ginny scoffed. "No. Never."

"But you make such a great pie," Lindsay joked. "I would think you'd have to fight them off with a stick."

"Keep peeling," Ginny admonished her. "There's also the sex, you know."

Lindsay looked confused. "But yesterday you said we weren't supposed to—"

Ginny's sharp glare cut her off. "You didn't have sex with him, did you?"

"No, ma'am."

Kaitlin shot Lindsay an expression of disbelief.

Lindsay returned a warning squint.

"Good girl," said Ginny, smiling all over again. "That was my problem. Always slept with them, never married them."

"You had lovers?" The question jumped out of Kaitlin before she could censor it. When Ginny was young, lovers must have been something scandalous.

"Dustin Cartwell," said Ginny on a sigh, getting a faraway look in her eyes as she dreamily cut the lard and shortening into the flour mixture inside the bowl. "And Michael O'Conner. Phillip Magneson. Oh, and that Anderson boy, Charlie."

"Go, Ginny," sang Lindsay.

"Never met one I wanted to keep," said Ginny with a shake of her white-haired head. "They fart, you know. Drop their underwear on the floor. And the snoring? Don't get me started on the snoring." She added another scoop of lard. "Now, we'll be making this half into chunks the size of peas. Keeps it flaky."

Kaitlin met Lindsay's gaze again, her body shaking with suppressed laughter. Ginny was an absolute blast.

Her attention abruptly off men and sex, and back onto the baking, she let each of them cut in some of the lard, then she showed them how to sprinkle on the water, keeping everything chilled. They rolled out the dough, cut it into pie pans, mixed the apples with cinnamon, sugar and corn starch, then made a latticework top.

In the end, both Kaitlin and Lindsay slid decent-looking pies into the oven.

"You don't want to be sharing that with Zachary," Ginny warned Kaitlin. Then she paused, a flash of confusion crossing her face. "Oh, my. You married him, didn't you?"

"I did," Kaitlin admitted. And after last night, the marriage was feeling frighteningly real.

Ginny patted her on the arm. "Wish you'd come and talked with me first."

"Is there something wrong with Zach?" Kaitlin couldn't help but ask. Ginny had been alluding to Zach's lack of desirability since they arrived.

"Those Harper boys are heartbreakers," said Ginny with a disapproving click of her tongue. "Always have been, always will be."

Kaitlin had to admit, she could easily see Zach breaking hearts. He'd been darn near perfect last night. He'd driven through the dark to rescue her from a storm, then made exquisite love to her, teased her and sympathized with her. If a woman were to let herself fall for a man like that, heartbreak might well be the inevitable outcome.

Ginny turned to Lindsay. "Now, my Dylan. That one's a catch. He's wealthy, you know."

"I do have my own money," said Lindsay.

Ginny chuckled and gave a coquettish smile. "A girl can never have too much money."

Lindsay was obviously puzzled. "You don't mind me marrying your great-nephew for his money?"

Ginny looked askance. "What other reason is there?"

Lindsay's brows went up. "Love?"

"Oh, pooh, pooh." Ginny waved a dismissive hand. "Love comes and goes. A bank balance, now there's something a gal can count on."

"Your lovers didn't have money?" Kaitlin asked, fascinated by Ginny's experiences and opinions.

A sly look entered Ginny's eyes, and once again she glanced around the kitchen as if checking for eavesdroppers. "They had youth and enthusiasm. I think they wanted *my* money."

"Do you have any pictures?" asked Lindsay, obviously as interested as Kaitlin in the older woman's love life.

"Indeed, I do." Ginny wiped her hands on the big apron,

ntying it from the back. Then she beckoned both women to ollow her as she made her way toward the kitchen door.

In the stairwell, Kaitlin asked, "Did the other Harper men reak women's hearts?"

"Every single one," Ginny confirmed with a decisive nod.

"But not their wives." Kaitlin's tone turned the statement into . question.

"Sometimes their wives, too."

"What about Sadie? Wasn't Sadie happy with Milton?"

"Milton was a fine man. He'd have made a good lover. But nce they were married, Sadie, she worried all the time."

"That he was unfaithful?" asked Kaitlin.

Ginny stopped midstair and turned on her. "Oh, no. A Harper nan would never be unfaithful." She turned and began climbing gain.

"Then why did Sadie worry?"

"She was the groundskeeper's daughter. Oh, she pretended all ight. But at her heart, she was never the mistress of the castle. 'hat's why she wouldn't make any changes."

They came to the second floor, and Ginny led them down a vide hallway. Overhead skylights let in the sunshine, while art bjects lined the shelves along the way.

"The castle is really beautiful," said Kaitlin. She wasn't sure he'd have changed anything, either.

"So was Sadie," said Ginny in a wistful voice. "Before Milton, ve swam naked in the ocean and ran across the sand under the ull moon."

"Do you really think he broke her heart?" Kaitlin persisted. Like Emma, Kaitlin really wanted to believe Sadie had been nappy here.

"No. Not really. But sometimes she felt trapped, and sometimes he worried." Ginny swept open the double doors of a closet. She noved aside a fluffy quilt and extracted a battered shoebox, pening it to reveal a stack of photographs. "Ah, here we are. Come meet my lovers."

Nine

Zach found Kaitlin in the portrait gallery, gazing at a painting of his grandmother when she had been in her twenties.

"Hey," he said, coming up behind her. He didn't ask and didn't wait for permission before wrapping his arms around her waist, nestling her into the cradle of his body.

"Do you think she was happy?" Kaitlin asked.

"Yes."

"Did you love your grandfather?"

"As far as I could tell." He hadn't spent much time looking at the portraits over the past years, and his memory of his grandmother was that of an old woman. He'd forgotten how lovely she was. No wonder his grandfather had married her so young.

"Ginny says she felt trapped sometimes."

"I love Ginny dearly," Zach began, a warning in his tone.

There was a thread of laughter in Kaitlin's voice when she interrupted him. "She doesn't seem too crazy about you."

"But you know she's not all there, right?"

"She's a blast," Kaitlin responded. "And her memory seems very sharp."

"Well, it had to be a pretty big cage. They went to Europe at least twice a year, and spent half their time in Manhattan. You should have seen the garden parties. The governor, theatre stars, foreign diplomats."

"Okay, so it was a big cage," Kaitlin conceded.

"Come here. Let me show you something." Zach shifted his arm around her shoulders, guiding her down the gallery toward the staircase.

"Your room?" she asked.

"No. But I like the way you're thinking." He steered her down to the first floor then back through the hallways to Sadie's parlor.

"What are we doing?"

"I want to show you that she was happy."

He sat Kaitlin on the settee and retrieved an old photo album from Sadie's bookcase. Sitting next to her, he flipped through the pages until he came to one of the Harpers' famous garden parties. The pictures were black and white, slightly faded, but they showed the gardens in their glory, and the sharp-dressed upper crust of New York nibbling finger sandwiches and chatting away the afternoon.

"That's her." Zach pointed to his grandmother in a flowing dress and a silk flower-brimmed hat. Her smile was bright, and Zach's grandfather Milton had a hand tucked against the small of her back.

"She does look happy," Kaitlin was forced to admit.

"And that's a hedge, not prison bars," said Zach.

Kaitlin elbowed him in the ribs. "The bars are meta-phorical."

"The hedge is real. So were the trips to Europe."

Kaitlin flipped the page, coming to more party photos, people laughing, drinking punch, playing croquet and wandering through the rose garden. There was a band in the gazebo, and a few couples were dancing on the patio. Some of the pictures showed children playing.

"That's my father," said Zack, smiling to himself as he pointed out the five-year-old boy in shorts, a white shirt and suspenders standing next to the duck pond. He had a rock in his hand, and one of his shoes was missing. He looked as if he was seconds away from wading after the ducks.

Kaitlin chuckled softly. "Were you anything like that as a child?"

Zach rose to retrieve another album.

"Here." He let her open it and page her way through the pictures of him as a young child.

"You were adorable," she cooed, moving from his toddler pictures to preschool to Zach at five years old, digging up flower bulbs, dirt smeared across his face and clothes.

"Yeah, let's go with adorable."

"Did you get into trouble for that?"

"I would guess I did. Probably from Grandma Sadie. Those gardens were her pride and joy."

"I never had a garden," said Kaitlin, and Zach immediately felt guilty for showing her the album. He'd done it again, parading out his past and his relatives without giving a thought to the contrast with her life.

"I bet you stayed cleaner than I did," he said, making a weak attempt at a joke.

"Once I realized—" She paused, gripping the edge of the album. "Hoo. I'm not going to do that." She turned another page.

"Do what?"

"Nothing." Her attention was focused on a series of shots of the beach and a picnic.

"Katie?"

"Nothing."

He gently removed the album from her hands. "I upset you."

"No, you didn't."

"Liar."

She straightened her shoulders. "It was hard, okay."

"I know."

"No, you don't."

"You're right. I don't." He folded the book closed and set it on the table beside him. "I'm sorry I showed you the photos. It was thoughtless."

"Don't worry about it."

"What were you going to say?"

She pasted him with a look of impatience.

"I've got all night to wait," he warned her, sitting back and making a show of getting comfortable.

She clenched her jaw, looking mulish, and he prepared himself for a contest of wills.

But then her toughness disappeared, and she swallowed. Then she closed her eyes for a second. "I was going to say…"

Part of him wanted to retract the question. But another part of him wanted to know, *needed* to know what she'd gone through as a child.

"I was going to say," she repeated, sounding small and fragile, "once I realized people could give me away." Her voice cracked. "I tried to be very, very good."

Zach honestly thought his heart was going to break.

He wrapped an arm around her and drew her close. She felt so tiny in his arms, so vulnerable. He hated that she'd been alone as a child.

"I'm sorry, Katie," he whispered against her hair.

She shook her head back and forth. "It's not your fault."

He drew a deep breath. "You've been alone for a very long time."

"I'm used to it."

But she wasn't. She couldn't be. Nobody should have to get used to not having a family. Zach had lost his parents when he was twenty, and that had been devastating enough. He'd still had his grandmother, and he'd always had the Gilbys. And he'd had Aunt Ginny, who usually liked him very much.

"Look," said Kaitlin, pulling back and wiping a single tear from her cheek. "There's a full moon outside."

He twisted his head to look out the window. "Yeah?"

"You want to go skinny-dipping?" she asked.

"Yes," he answered without hesitation.

* * *

The salt water was chilly against Kaitlin's skin, but Zach's body felt deliciously warm. He held her flush against himself, her feet dangling just above the sandy bottom. Over his left shoulder, she could see the distant lights of the Gilby house. And when she turned her head the other way, she could see the Harper castle in all its glory.

The gardens were smaller than they were in the pictures, but they were still lit up at night. And an illuminated path wound its way from the edge of the garden to the sandy beach, where she and Zach had stripped off their clothes before plunging into the surf.

"Lindsay is talking about staying a few more days," Zach offered.

Kaitlin drew back to look at him. "With Dylan?" Lindsay hadn't said anything to her. Then again, she had spent most of her time at the Gilby house.

Zach's teeth flashed white under the moonlight. "I think they have worked out their differences."

"You mean Lindsay won," Kaitlin corrected. "Where's my ten dollars, by the way?"

"Dylan thinks he's the one who won."

"He totally caved."

"I don't think he cares."

"By the way, if Ginny asks, they're not having sex."

"Ohhh-kay," Zach slowly agreed.

"She'll probably ask," Kaitlin warned. "She's obsessed with Dylan's love life."

"I won't answer," Zach pledged.

"Good."

Neither Kaitlin nor Zach spoke for a few minutes. The cool waves bobbed their bodies, while the sound of the surf rushed up on the sand, punctuating the breeze that whispered through the bushes along the shoreline.

"You want to stay, too?" Zach asked softly, rocking her back and forth in his arms.

Kaitlin stilled against him, not sure what he was asking.

"With Lindsay?" he elaborated. "For a few days? You could work right from here?"

"What about you?" she asked, still wondering what he meant by the invitation. Was he asking her to stay on the island, or to stay with him?

"If you're staying?" A slow, sultry smiled curved his mouth, darkening his eyes to slate. "I'm sure not leaving."

Kaitlin's smile grew in return. "Okay."

"Yeah?"

"Yes."

He spun her in a circle, and she wrapped her legs around his waist, her hands gripping his shoulders for balance. His hold was tight under her bottom as she knifed through the water.

The moon glistened high in the sky, surrounded by layers of stars. They were the same stars that Lyndall had used to navigate his way to the island hundreds of years ago. The same stars that Sadie had gazed at as a girl and as a woman, a mother.

Zach slowed and stopped, the waves now the only motion around them. Kaitlin gazed at the lighted gardens that Sadie had so clearly loved. The woman had been the guardian of the castle, the keeper of the family's heritage. And because of her decisions, Kaitlin had been trusted with the Harper office building.

Zach nuzzled her neck.

The office building was much newer, of course. But Kaitlin couldn't help but believe the renovations would matter to Sadie. Maybe Zach was right. Maybe wholesale change wasn't such a great thing. Maybe Kaitlin had some kind of responsibility to his family.

Maybe she needed to rethink her approach.

"Zach?" she ventured.

"Hmm?" he asked, the vibration of his lips tickling the sensitized skin of her neck.

"Could you get me a copy of the Hugo Rosche plans?"

He drew back, brows going up. "Really?"

"Yes."

"Sure." He nodded, the nod growing faster. "Of course I could."

"I'm not making any promises," she warned him.

"I understand."

"I'm just going to look." She had no idea what she was going to do now. She still needed her career, which meant she needed a fantastic project for the Harper building. But maybe there was a compromise of some kind. She just didn't know.

A smile curved Zach's mouth. "No problem."

"I don't want you to get your hopes up."

"Oh, Katie." He planted a long, warm kiss on her damp mouth. He drew back, his grin wide as he smoothed her hair. "My hopes have been up for quite some time now."

She gave in to her desire for him, tipping her head and giving her lashes a few flirtatious blinks. "And what exactly are you hoping for?"

"You. Naked."

She made a show of glancing at their bodies. "I'm liking your chances."

"In my pirate's lair." He kissed her neck once more, then her jawline, her cheek, working his way to the corner of her mouth.

"Piece of advice, Zach?"

"Speed things up?" he asked hopefully, and she couldn't help but laugh.

"For future reference, that line will probably be a lot more successful if you refer to it as a castle instead of a lair."

His hand closed over her breast, peaked and sensitized in the cool, damp air.

She gasped at the sensation.

"Lair," he repeated on a growl.

"Fine. Yes. Whatever."

Three days later, Dylan's parents arrived, back from their business meetings in Chicago. And, as usual, they brought company.

Zach was happy to see them. David and Darcie were two of his favorite people in the world. After his parents died, they'd become even more important in his life. David was a brilliant businessman, while Darcie was the most loving and compassionate honorary aunt Zach could have wished for.

Still, he knew this meant the end of his interlude with Kaitlin. Dylan would never have a woman stay at the house with his parents there, and it was past time for Zach to get back to Manhattan.

"You weren't kidding about them having a few friends over," Kaitlin observed as they drove the golf cart the last quarter mile to the Gilbys' house. Music wafted from the open windows, and it was easy to see groups of people circulating on the deck.

"What are the Gilbys like?"

"David's savvy, hardworking, a great guy to go to for advice. Darcie's friendly, gregarious. You'll like her."

"What will she think of me…?" Kaitlin's voice trailed off on the half-finished question.

He put his hand over hers. "We can let her think whatever you like." He paused, but Kaitlin didn't step in and offer a suggestion. "How about a business associate and a friend?" he asked.

Kaitlin accepted with a smile.

Zach fought a shot of disappointment, but he let it slide. He didn't want people to think Kaitlin was his business associate. He wanted them to think… He paused. What? That she was his lover? His girlfriend? His wife? His hands gripped tighter on the steering wheel. He was going to have to figure it out. Not right this minute, of course. But soon.

"Lindsay will probably stay at my place for the night," he told Kaitlin. "When it's only Ginny, well, she'd never notice. But with his parents, Dylan doesn't…"

"I understand," Kaitlin said, nodding easily.

Zach hoped Lindsay would react the same way.

Then again, that was Dylan's problem. Zach's problem was figuring out where things were left with him and Kaitlin.

Would they continue seeing each other in Manhattan? He had quickly grown used to waking up with her every morning. He liked having her around for breakfast, reconnecting over dinner. Hell, he wasn't even sure he wanted to sign the damn divorce papers anymore.

Of course, that was ridiculous.

Luckily, that decision was months away.

He glanced at Kaitlin's profile, taking in her pert nose, those gorgeous green eyes, the spray of freckles that had come out in the sun. And, of course, her wild, coconut-scented auburn hair that he buried his face into every chance he got.

At the top of the driveway, he pressed the button to open the garage door, pulling the golf cart inside, unable to shake the feeling that something precious had just ended.

He stepped out and rounded the vehicle. Then he took Kaitlin's hand, leading her to the three steps and the doorway that would take them into the house and the party.

Unable to help himself, he stopped her there, cradled her face in his hands and kissed her thoroughly.

She responded, like she always did, soft lips parted, a light touch of her tongue meshing with his. Her breasts pressed up against his chest, and she came up on her toes to meet him partway. He loved that about her.

His arms tightened around her slender waist.

This wasn't goodbye, he told himself. She worked for him, with him. They'd both be in Manhattan. They would see each other at the office every day.

Hell, they were *married*. She couldn't just run off and disappear from his life. He'd find a way to keep her with him for a long time to come.

She pulled back. "You keep this up, and they're never going to believe we're business colleagues."

"We're husband and wife," he said gruffly.

She grinned and playfully swiped her index finger across the tip of his nose. "We're pretty much faking everything here, aren't we, Zach?"

He opened his mouth to protest, but she turned away, skipping up the stairs, opening the door and ending the moment.

He quickly trapped the door with his hand before it could swing shut. Music chimed from the sound system, while chattering voices spilled from the deck into the great room. All the staff members were working, impeccably dressed and serving drinks or circulating with appetizers.

Zach knew the kitchen would be a hive of activity. He also knew Ginny would be in her element, visiting with guests into the evening until she gave in to exhaustion. He saw Kaitlin heading toward Lindsay on the deck and started after her.

"Zach," came David's booming voice. "Great to see you at home, son."

"Welcome back, sir." Zach shook his hand.

"You remember Kevin O'Connor." David gestured to a fiftyish gentleman with a three-olive martini in his hand.

"Swiss International Bank," Zach acknowledged, shaking again, checking for Kaitlin out the corner of his eye.

"Kevin has a client," David began. "He's out of Hong Kong, and he's got mining interests in Canada and South America."

"I see," Zach said, dutifully focusing his attention. Mining companies were massive shippers; ore was both heavy and voluminous. And a Hong Kong client likely had access to the mainland China market. Zach's personal life would have to go on hold for a moment.

The moment turned into half an hour. A drink was put into Zach's hand, and a third man joined them, a friend of Kevin's with an interest in manufacturing.

By the time the conversation wound down, Kaitlin was nowhere to be found. Neither was Lindsay.

He managed to track down Dylan, who was with Ginny, then he was rewarded when he heard Kaitlin's voice from behind him.

"You must be enjoying the party," she offered breezily to Ginny, who was decked out in chiffon and diamonds, a folded, lace fan in her hand and her dogs at her feet in rhinestone collars.

"And who is this young lady?" Ginny asked in an imperious tone. She leaned toward Kaitlin. "Are you here with my grandson? He's a catch, you know."

Zach turned in time to see Kaitlin's surprise morph into obvious disappointment.

"I'd stay away from this one," said Ginny, tapping Zach's arm with the fan. "He's a reprobate and a heartbreaker."

Kaitlin's eyes clouded to jade.

"Auntie—" Dylan stepped in "—this is Kaitlin Saville and Lindsay Rubin."

"Pretty," Ginny acknowledged with a gracious sweep of her fan.

"Kaitlin is my architect," said Zach.

Ginny looked at him, eyes clouding with puzzlement. "Are you changing the castle? Does Sadie know?"

There was an instant and awkward silence.

Zack had been through this before, about a dozen times so far, but it never got any easier.

He gently took Ginny's hand and lowered his tone. "Aunt Ginny, do you remember that Sadie passed away?"

Ginny drew back warily. Then she gave herself a little shake. "Of *course* I remember. I meant…" Her voice trailed off.

Dylan stepped in again. "Auntie, would you like to dance?"

Ginny snapped him with her fan, seeming to recover. "I'm too old to dance. People my age are dropping like flies." Her attention turned to Lindsay. "You should dance with my grandson. He has a lot of money."

Darcie joined the circle, and Zach took the opportunity to whisk Kaitlin away.

"You okay?" he asked as they made their way out onto the deck. The sun had set, and the lights were coming on all over the grounds. The music seemed to swell louder, and the conversation grew more animated as the guests consumed martinis, wine and single malt.

"She didn't remember me at all." Sadness was clear in Kaitlin's tone as they came to the rail.

"She will," Zach promised, not sure if he was lying or not. Ginny's early memories were her best. Recent events often escaped her.

"She taught me to bake pie." Kaitlin's voice was stilted. She leaned her arms on the railing and stared out at the ocean. "Nobody ever taught me to bake before. I was starting to think…"

She paused, then tried a lukewarm smile. "I'm being silly. She's old. Of course she forgets things. You were great."

"I didn't do anything."

"How many times have you had to tell her about your grandmother?"

"A few," Zach admitted. And he was sure that previous one wouldn't be the last. He stared at the lights at his place, wishing they were down there right now.

"Kaitlin?" Ginny's voice surprised Zach. "There you are, dear." She sidled up to Kaitlin, glancing warily around them, her voice becoming conspiratorial. "I've changed my mind."

Kaitlin's smile was bright as she blinked away the telltale sheen in her eyes. "You have?"

"That nice girl, Lindsay?"

Kaitlin nodded, and Zach smiled in relief.

"I think she should sleep with Dylan."

"What?"

Ginny placed a hand on Kaitlin's arm. "Hear me out." Then she turned and gave Zach a censorious look. "Excuse us please, Zachary. The women would like to talk."

Zach held his palms up in surrender and backed away.

He circulated through the party a little, and then Dylan caught up with him outside David's study and herded him inside to where they were alone.

Dylan seemed agitated. He crossed to the small bar and poured himself a scotch. "You okay to take Lindsay down with you tonight?"

"No problem."

Dylan waggled a second, empty glass, raising his brow to Zach in question.

"Sure," Zach answered, walking farther into the room, the noise of the party fading behind him through the open door.

"I haven't told her yet," Dylan confessed, handing Zach a crystal tumbler of single malt then taking a sip from his own.

"You need my help?"

Dylan shook his head, moving to the bay window. "She'll be disappointed. At least, I hope she'll be disappointed. But she's a trouper. She really is, Zach. She's quite the little trouper." He took another sip.

Zach moved closer. "Are you okay?"

"Sure. Fine. Why?"

Zach had never seen Dylan act this way, not over a woman, not over anything. "Something going on between you and Lindsay? I mean, other than the obvious?"

"What's the obvious?"

Treading on unfamiliar ground, Zach chose his words carefully. "A physical...connection?"

"Oh, yeah. That."

"But there's more," Zach guessed.

Dylan shot him a look that questioned his sanity, but Zach had no idea how to interpret it. Was there something serious going on between Dylan and Lindsay? Had he made her angry again?

"I should warn you," said Zach, stepping into the silence. "Aunt Ginny is out there advising Lindsay to sleep with you."

Dylan stilled. *"What?"*

"I assume it's to trap you into marriage. You might want to watch your back."

"I don't think it's my back that needs watching," Dylan muttered.

"You don't seem too worried."

Dylan shrugged.

Zach watched his friend's expression carefully. "Seriously, Dylan. Is there something going on between you two?"

Dylan frowned. "I'm not saying there is."

"Are you saying there's not?"

Dylan compressed his lips. "What about you and Kaitlin?" he asked, turning the tables.

"Nothing," Zach lied, perching on the arm of an overstuffed leather chair. He wasn't ready to talk to anybody about his relationship with Kaitlin. He didn't even have it straight in his own mind yet.

"You're sleeping with her," said Dylan.

Zach shot him a pointed look. "That's just..." In fact, Zach wasn't sure exactly what it was. Somehow his physical attraction to Kaitlin, their renovation battle and their mock marriage had all meshed together in a way that was well past confusing.

"Sex?" Dylan asked bluntly.

"It's not relevant," said Zach.

"What about the renovation? Is that relevant? You haven't forgotten why she's here, have you?"

"No, I haven't forgotten why she's here."

Dylan took another drink. "So, the plan's working?"

"It's going great," Zach admitted, trying to inject some enthusiasm for how well things were working out for him on that front. "She asked for the Hugo Rosche plans. She's been using them for the past few days. And, well, I think she's getting that Grandma Sadie wasn't progressive and flamboyant. And she's figuring it out for herself, which is exactly what we wanted."

"So, your devious little scheme is coming together in spades," Dylan summed up.

"It was *your* devious little scheme."

"You approved it," Dylan noted. "You implemented it. And it looks like you'll save yourself a bundle."

"I did," Zach agreed. Too bad saving a bundle didn't seem so important anymore. Too bad he'd started to wish he *could* give Kaitlin her dream project, unlimited funds, unfettered imagination.

"I think we've heard just about enough," Lindsay's lawyer voice cut in.

Zach whirled, nearly spilling his drink.

In the study's open doorway stood Kaitlin, her face completely pale.

Lindsay's face was beet-red.

Dylan had turned to a statue.

"You—" Lindsay pointed to Dylan, anger quaking deep in her voice "—scheming little pirate-boy. You take us back to Manhattan, right this minute."

Ten

The next afternoon, Kaitlin struggled to forget the entire weekend. If she chalked up her experience on Serenity Island to yet another childish fantasy where she found a family and lived happily ever after, she could cope with the way Zach had systematically and deliberately ripped her heart out.

It wasn't real.

It had never been real.

Working from her apartment, she'd gone back to her original renovation designs, ignoring the twinges of guilt when she thought about Ginny and Sadie and what they might think of what she was doing to the Harpers' Manhattan building.

This wasn't about Sadie, nor was it about the Harper and Gilby families. This was about Kaitlin, and her career, and her ability to stand on her own two feet and take care of herself every second of every day for the rest of her life.

So despite the knowledge that Sadie was unlikely to approve of the three extra floors, the five-story lobby, the saltwater aquarium and the palm trees, those features were staying, every single one of them. And she'd added a helipad. Who knew when Dylan would want to drop in?

She'd even thought about replacing the fountains in the lobby with a two-story waterfall. In fact, she was still considering it.

It was halfway through the afternoon, and her legs were starting to cramp. She rose from her computer, crossing the living room to the kitchen, snagging her second Sugar Bob's doughnut. She knew they were becoming an addiction. But she promised herself she'd add an extra half hour at the gym every day, and she'd kick the habit completely just as soon as the Harper building renovation was complete.

A woman could only handle so many things at once. She took a big bite.

There was a rap on her door, so she ditched the doughnut in the box and tossed the box back into her cupboard, wiping the powdered sugar from her lips.

For a split second she wondered if it might be Zach. Then, just as quickly, she promised herself she wouldn't open the door if it was.

She wouldn't.

She had absolutely nothing left to say to the man.

But when she checked through the peephole, it was Lindsay standing in the hallway. Kaitlin opened the door to find her friend balancing a large Agapitos pizza box on one hand and holding a bottle of tequila in the other.

"Pepperoni and sausage," Lindsay said without preamble, walking forward as Kaitlin opened the door up wide and shifted out of the way. "I hope you have limes."

It was only three-thirty. Somewhat early to start in on margaritas, but the day was already a nutritional bust, so what the hell?

"How are you holding up?" asked Lindsay as she crossed to the small kitchen table while Kaitlin shut and latched the apartment door.

"I am absolutely fine," said Kaitlin, her determination putting a spring in her step as she squared her shoulders.

"You are a terrible liar," Lindsay countered.

That was true enough. But Kaitlin also knew that if she said something loud enough and often enough, sometimes it started to feel true.

Kaitlin headed for the fridge, reciting the words she'd rehearsed in her mind. "So it turned out to be a con. It wasn't like we didn't expect it to be one. Zach was fighting to save money. I was fighting for my career. Our positions were incompatible from the get-go." She paused, taking a moment to regroup her emotions. "Though I have to admit, I didn't expect him to be quite so good."

She tugged open the fridge door, fighting to keep her voice even, but not doing a particularly good job. "Still, I was colossally stupid to have fallen for his act. I mean, didn't you and I call it almost to the detail before we left?"

"I never thought he'd take it as far as he did," Lindsay ventured from behind her.

"I did," said Kaitlin with a decisive nod as she bent to scoop a couple of limes from the crisper drawer. "He was trying to use sex as an advantage all along."

She'd known that. And she had no idea why she'd let herself sink so far into a ridiculous fantasy. She'd figured it out, yet in four short days he had her convinced to do exactly what he'd wanted with the renovations, and she was romping wantonly in his bed every night to boot.

Stupid move.

She snagged the limes.

Yesterday she'd been angry.

This morning she'd been heartbroken.

Right now, she was more embarrassed than anything.

"What about you?" she asked Lindsay, making up her mind to quit talking about it as she closed the fridge.

"What about me?" Lindsay had perched herself on one of the stools at the small breakfast bar with the pizza box in front of her.

Kaitlin set the limes down on the countertop and pulled a long, sharp knife out of the wooden block. "What about you and Dylan?"

"There is no me and Dylan."

"There was yesterday."

Lindsay gave her blond hair a quick toss. "He's dead to me."

"I like that," Kaitlin said defiantly, slicing into a lime. It sounded so unemotional and final.

"Have you heard anything from Zach?" Lindsay asked.

Kaitlin squeezed half a lime into the blender as she shook her head. "If I see his number, I'll hang up. And if he drops by, I won't answer the door."

"What about the renovation?"

Kaitlin emphasized her words by pointing the knife tip to her computer on the dining table. "I am doing my full-blown design. I'm adding a helipad and a waterfall. It'll be fabulous. I'll probably win an award."

Lindsay flipped open the cardboard box, folding it back to reveal the gooey, fragrant pizza. "I can't believe they turned out to be such rats."

"Dead-to-us rats," Kaitlin stated, fighting to keep her emotions in check over the thought of never seeing Zach again.

Why had she let herself trust him? Did she think he'd love her, really marry her, have babies with her and turn her life into some fantasy?

She was Kaitlin Saville, penniless orphan. Things like that didn't happen to her.

Lindsay tore a bite from one of the pizza slices and popped it into her mouth. "You thought he was the one?" she ventured softly.

Suddenly exhausted, Kaitlin set down the knife. "Stupid of me, I know."

"It's not your fault."

"It's all my fault."

"He played you."

"And I let him. I encouraged him. I helped him. And now all I have left is revenge."

"Revenge can be satisfying," said Lindsay. "Especially when it's going to save your career."

"I don't want revenge," Kaitlin responded with blunt honesty, turning to squeeze the other half of the lime into the blender. "I hate revenge. I feel like I'm getting revenge against Sadie instead of Zach." She dropped the lime peel and braced herself against the countertop.

She knew she couldn't do it.

She couldn't spend Harper money on a design she knew Sadie would hate. Her laugh sounded more like a cry.

"Katie?" Lindsay was up and rounding the breakfast bar.

"I'm fine," Kaitlin sniffed. But she wasn't fine. She was about to give up her career and her future for a family that wasn't even hers.

"Don't you love it when you know you've been a jerk?" Dylan asked, cupping his hands behind his head and stretching back in the padded chair next to Zach's office window.

Zach was standing, too restless to sit down while his mind struggled to settle on a course of action.

"I mean," Dylan continued, "sometimes you're not sure. But other times, like this, you're positive you've been a complete ass."

Zach folded his arms across his chest, watching the clouds streak across the sky far away over the Jersey shore. "Are you talking about me or you?"

"I'm talking about both of us."

Zach turned. He didn't know about Dylan's behavior, but he maintained that he'd been put in an untenable position. He never set out to hurt anyone. He was only trying to do right by his company and his family.

"And what should I have done differently?" he demanded.

Dylan grinned at Zach's upset. "I don't know. Maybe you shouldn't have pretended you were married."

"I *am* married."

"I'm guessing not for long."

Zach shook his head. "She's not going to divorce me. It's her leverage."

At least he hoped Kaitlin wasn't going to divorce him yet. He wasn't ready for that.

Dylan crossed an ankle over one knee. "Conning her into scaling back the renovation was one thing. But you're not a heartless bastard, Zach. Why'd you mess with her emotions like that?"

Zach felt his anger rise. What he'd done with Kaitlin was none of Dylan's business. It was between him and Kaitlin. It was... They were...

"And what about you?" he queried, deflecting the question. "You slept with Lindsay."

"That was a simple fling."

"And what do you think I had?"

Dylan sat up straight. "I don't know, Zach. You tell me." His gaze moved meaningfully to the package of papers on the table between them.

"That's nothing," Zach denied. That was simply him being a decent human being, something which Dylan didn't seem to believe was possible.

"You put nine private investigators on the case."

"So?" Zach had wanted something fast. More men, better speed.

"So how did that benefit you?"

"It wasn't supposed to benefit me." It was meant to benefit Kaitlin, to put a smile on her face, to banish the haunted look that came into her eyes every time the subject of his family came up, which was nearly every second they were on Serenity Island.

But the effort had pretty much been a failure. Despite the high-end manpower, all he'd found of Kaitlin's heritage was a grainy old newspaper photo showing her grandparents and her mother as a young girl. The family home had burned down, killing the grandparents and destroying all of the family possessions when Kaitlin's mother was sixteen, two years before Kaitlin was born.

The picture, two names and a gravesite were all Zach had turned up.

"You still going to give them to her?" asked Dylan.

"Sure," said Zach, with a shrug, pretending it was no big deal. "Maybe I'll mail them over."

"Mail them?"

"Mail them."

"You don't want to see her in person?"

Zach bristled. "To do what? To say what? To let her yell at me again?" Truth was, he'd give anything to see Kaitlin again, even if it was only to hear her yell. But what was the point? He'd chewed up her trust and spit it out, over and over again.

"You could tell her you sold the ship."

"Big deal." So Zach had come up with seventy-five million dollars. It wasn't as if he had a choice. Kaitlin would be full steam ahead on the renovation again, and the only way he was going to get his company back was to give her the carte blanche she'd demanded. The only way to do that was to sell an asset. So he'd sold an asset. She wouldn't give him brownie points for doing that. "You think an old newspaper photo and money I had to give her all along are going to make a difference?"

"You gotta try, Zach."

"No, I don't."

"You're in love with her."

"No, I'm not."

Dylan coughed out a cold laugh and came to his feet. "You sorry son-of-a—"

"I am not in love with Kaitlin."

He liked Kaitlin. Sure, he liked Kaitlin. What was not to like?

And, yeah, he'd have stayed with her for the foreseeable future. He'd have woken up next to her for as long as she'd let him. And maybe for a few days there he'd entertained fantasies about what could happen between them long term.

But those were just fantasies. They had nothing to do with the real world.

In the real world, he and Kaitlin were adversaries. She'd wanted to save her career, and he'd wanted to keep his company intact. She'd won. He'd lost. Nothing to be done about it now but mop up after the fallout.

"I saw your face when she walked out," Dylan offered. "I've known you your whole life, Zach."

Zach turned on him. "You know *nothing*."

"You're going to lie to me? That's your next big plan?"

"I don't have a next big plan."

"Well, you'd better come up with one. Or you're going to lose Kaitlin forever."

The words felt like a stake in Zach's heart.

He didn't love Kaitlin. He couldn't love Kaitlin. It would be a disaster to love Kaitlin.

He swallowed.

"What about you?" he asked Dylan.

"I already have a plan," Dylan stated with smug satisfaction. "And I don't even love Lindsay. I'm just not ready to let her go yet."

"That's how it starts," said Zach.

Dylan's brows shot up. "And you know this because…?"

"What's your plan?" Zach countered.

Okay, maybe he did love Kaitlin just a little bit. But he'd get over it.

"I'm kidnapping Lindsay. She wanted a pirate, she's getting a pirate. Can I borrow your yacht?"

"You can't kidnap her."

"Watch me."

Zach took in the determination in Dylan's eyes. And for a second there, he wished he could simply kidnap Kaitlin. If he could get her on board his yacht, he could probably keep her there for a few days, maybe even a few weeks. By the end of it, like Lyndall, he might be able to win her over.

On the other hand, she might have him arrested. Or she might throw him overboard. Or she might decide the Harper building needed to be a hundred stories high and truly bankrupt him.

Kidnapping was not a real option.

Instead, he'd give her the money. He'd give her the news clipping and the photo. Then, like the gentleman he'd once been, he'd step out of her life forever.

* * *

Three margaritas later, Kaitlin splashed cold water on her face in the small bathroom of her apartment. She and Lindsay had started to giggle about half an hour back, but now she found herself fighting tears.

It didn't seem to matter that Zach had played her for a fool. She'd fallen in love with him, and no matter how many times she told herself it was all a lie, she couldn't stop wanting the man she'd known on Serenity Island.

She dried her face and ran a comb through her hair, gathering her frayed emotions. Much as she wished she could drink herself into oblivion today, it was time to stop wallowing in self-pity and get her equilibrium back.

Her career in New York was over. Truthfully, she might as well walk away from the Harper project altogether. What Sadie and Zach would want wouldn't do a thing to save Kaitlin's career.

At least most of her boxes were still packed.

Another tear leaked out, and she impatiently swiped it away. She told herself she was tough, and she was strong, and she was independent. And she would salvage her life or die trying.

She left the bathroom at a determined pace, rounding the bedroom door into the living room. There, her steps staggered to a stop.

Zach stood in the middle of her apartment, large as life and twice as sexy.

She was too stunned to shriek, too stunned to cry, too stunned to do anything, but let her jaw drop open.

"Hello, Kaitlin."

She still didn't have her bearings. "Huh?"

"I came to apologize."

She glanced swiftly around the apartment. "Where's Lindsay? How did you—?"

"Lindsay left with Dylan."

Kaitlin gave her head a little shake, but she wasn't delusional. That really was Zach standing there. "Why would she do that?"

"He kidnapped her," said Zach. "I wouldn't expect to see her for a few days."

"He can't do that."

"That's what I said," Zach agreed. "But I don't think those two have ever cared much about the rules."

"Lindsay's a lawyer." Of course she cared about the rules. She was passionate about the rules.

Zach seemed to ponder that fact for a few moments. "Yeah," he conceded. "Dylan may have a bit of a problem with that when he brings her back."

"Is that a joke?" Was Lindsay about to jump out of the closet?

Instead of answering, Zach took a few steps forward. Her heart rate increased. Her chest went tight. And a low buzz started in the base of her belly.

She knew she should fight the reaction, but she had no idea how to turn it off.

"He took my yacht," said Zach, moving closer still, his gaze locked with hers every step of the way.

"So you're an accessory to kidnapping?" Her shock at the sight of him was starting to wear off, replaced by amazement that he was actually standing here in front of her. She could feel herself sink reluctantly back into the fantasy.

"Dylan told me she wanted a pirate, so she was getting a pirate."

"Is that why you're here?" she asked. "To help Dylan?"

"No."

"Then why?"

"Because I have something for you."

She forced herself to go cold and demanding. "I hope it's a big check." She knew she'd given up, abandoned the renovation, but Zach didn't need to know that yet.

"As a matter of fact, it is."

"Good." She gave a decisive nod, marveling at her own ability to hold her composure. The urge to throw herself into Zach's arms grew more powerful by the second.

"Seventy-five million dollars," he told her.

It took a few seconds for his words to sink in.

"What?" She took a reflexive step back.

"I sold a ship."

"What?"

"I'm giving you seventy-five million dollars for the renovation."

Kaitlin blinked at him.

"But that's not the real reason I'm here."

For a split second, hope flared within her. But she squelched it. Zach couldn't be trusted. She'd learned that the hard way half a dozen times over.

He handed her an envelope. "I'm here to give you this. It's not much."

Watching him warily, Kaitlin lifted the flap. She slid out a laminated picture. It showed a twentysomething couple with a young, blonde girl at the beach. The caption was *Holiday Travelers Enjoy Fourth of July Celebrations.*

She didn't understand.

"Phillipe and Aimee Saville," Zach said softly, and it felt as if Kaitlin's heart stopped.

"It was the best I could do," he continued. "There was a house fire in 1983. None of their possessions were saved. But the private investigators found this in the archives of a New Jersey newspaper. The little girl is your mother."

Kaitlin was completely speechless.

Her grandparents?

Zach had found grandparents?

Zach had *looked* for her grandparents?

Her fingers reflexively tightened on the photograph, and she felt herself sway to one side.

Zach's hand closed around her shoulder, steadying her.

"I've had three margaritas," she told him, embarrassed. She ought to be completely sober for a moment like this.

"That explains why Lindsay went so quietly."

Kaitlin fought against the sensation of his touch, even as she struggled to make sense of his gesture. "How? Where?" *Why* had he done this?

"I had some people start looking last week. After you told me." His hand tightened on her shoulder. "And I couldn't stand to see the pain in your eyes."

Her throat closed tighter, and her chest burned with emotion. She had to blink back tears at his thoughtfulness. Her voice dropped to a pained whisper. "How am I supposed to hate you?"

He drew a deep breath. Then he closed his eyes for a long second. He reached out and gently smoothed her hair back from her forehead. "You're not."

His hand stayed there, resting against her hair. Her nerves tingled where he touched. Her body begged her to sway forward against him, even as her mind ordered her to hold still.

She couldn't trust him. She didn't trust him. Oh, my, how she wanted to trust him.

He stroked his way to her cheek, cupping her face, tilting his head at an angle she'd come to recognize, to love.

He was going to kiss her, just like he'd done a hundred times, maybe a thousand. His lips dipped closer, and she moistened her own. She inhaled his scent, and her body relaxed into the exquisite moment.

"You're not supposed to hate me," he repeated on a whisper. "You're supposed to love me."

Then, he paused with his lips just barely brushing hers. "Because I love you, Katie. I love you so much."

His mouth captured hers, sending joy cascading through her body. His kiss was deep, sweet and long. His arms wrapped fully around her, hauling her close, pulling her safely into the circle of his embrace.

She clung to him, molding against him, passion and joy making her feel weightless.

After long minutes, he finally drew back. "Renovate anything you want," he rasped. "I'll sell half the damn fleet if I have to. Just don't leave me again. Not ever."

"I gave up the new design," she told him.

He drew back. "What? Why?"

"Sadie wouldn't like it."

Zach stilled. "Sadie doesn't matter. The past doesn't matter. Only the future, Kaitlin. And you're the future. You're *my* future."

Kaitlin's heart soared at the thought of a future with Zach—such a loving, thoughtful man.

Her voice quavered as she spoke. "You found my grandparents."

"I did," he acknowledged. "I know they were buried in New Jersey."

"You know where they're buried?"

"Yes."

Twin tears rolled from Kaitlin's eyes at that. "Have I mentioned that I love you?"

"No." He shook his head. "You hadn't. And I was getting worried."

"Well, I do."

"Thank goodness." He drew a deep breath, tightening his arms around her. "I told Dylan to give me an hour. Otherwise, you were getting kidnapped, too."

"You would not."

"Hell, yes, I would. One way or another, you and I are starting on a whole new generation of Harper pirates."

Kaitlin smiled at his joke, her body sighing in contentment. "Sadie would be pleased."

"Yes, she would," Zach agreed. "She'd also be gloating over the success of her scheme. In fact, I can almost hear her chuckling from here."

Kaitlin moved her hand to take another look at the picture of her grandparents. Her grandfather was tall. Her grandmother slightly rounded with light, curly hair. And her mother looked bright-eyed and happy with a shovel and pail in her hands. "I can't believe you did this."

"We can go visit their graves." He paused. "I swapped Dylan the yacht for a helicopter. It's standing by."

Kaitlin was overwhelmed by this thoughtfulness. But she wasn't anywhere near ready to leave his arms.

She molded her body to his. "Or maybe we could go in an hour or so?"

He sucked in a breath, lifting the picture from her hand and setting it safely on an end table. Then his eyes darkened, and he bent forward to kiss her thoroughly.

"Maybe in an hour or so," he agreed and scooped her up to head for her bedroom.

Epilogue

Following a month-long kidnapping, Lindsay and Dylan's wedding was held on Serenity Island, on the emerald-green lawn at the Gilby house, next to the pool. The bride was radiant, the groom ecstatic and the guests a who's who of New York City. According to Ginny, it was the biggest party the island had held since the heyday of the 1940s.

Dylan had insisted on flying the Jolly Roger, while Ginny confided gleefully to Kaitlin that since the wedding was so rushed, she wondered if Lindsay might be pregnant.

After the toasts were made, the five-tiered cake was cut and the dancing had started in the late afternoon, Zach drew Kaitlin to one side.

"There's something I need to show you," he told her quietly, tugging her inside the house and down the hallway toward the garage.

"We can't leave now," she protested, trotting on her high heels, the glossy, champagne-colored bridesmaid dress flowing around her knees.

"We'll be back in a few minutes," he assured her, opening the garage door.

"Zach," she protested.

"What?"

"Are you crazy?"

He turned and playfully kissed the tip of her nose. "Crazy for you."

"This isn't a joke." She tried to sound stern, but she didn't seem capable of getting angry with him. Since the afternoon in her apartment, and their helicopter trip to the cemetery to put roses on her grandparents' graves, she'd been almost giddy with love.

He braced his hand against the passenger side of a golf cart. "And I'm not laughing. Hop in."

"I will not hop in." She crossed her arms stubbornly over her chest. She wasn't abandoning Lindsay on her wedding day.

"Have it your way." He gently but firmly deposited her on the narrow bench seat.

"Hey!" She scrambled to get her dress organized around herself.

"There's something I really have to show you." He jumped into the driver's side and turned on the key.

Before she could escape, the cart pulled smoothly out of the garage onto the gravel driveway and the road that led down to the castle.

"I can't believe you're kidnapping me," she harrumphed.

"It is the pirate way."

"You are *not* allowed to ravish me in the middle of a wedding reception." She smoothed her dress over her knees and put her nose primly in the air.

Zach gave her a wolfish grin, and she was forced to wonder which one of them would prevail if push came to shove, and he did decide he wanted to ravish her.

They drove all the way down to the Harper property.

As they entered the castle gardens, she felt herself relax. This had quickly become one of her favorite places in the world. It was filled with such history and such happy memories.

Zach pulled to a halt in front of the family chapel, then he hopped out and came around to assist her.

She shook her head in confusion as she clambered around the awkward dress. It was made for fashion, not mobility. The bodice was tight, coming to a drop waist, while the satin skirt billowed out with crinolines, ending at knee length. "This is what you wanted to show me?" She'd been in the gardens a thousand times.

"Have patience," he told her.

"I'll have patience after the reception. Seriously, Zach. We have to get back."

But he led her by the hand to the bottom of the chapel steps.

"What are we doing?" she breathed in frustration.

A secretive smile growing on his lips, he reached into his tux jacket pocket and drew something out, holding his palm flat so that she could focus on a small heirloom ring.

It was a delicately swirled gold band, with a sapphire center, flanked by diamonds.

"I don't know how old it is," said Zach. "But I think it might have belonged to Lyndall."

"Stolen?" Kaitlin asked, glancing up.

"Let's assume not." Zach's silver eyes sparkled. He held her hand in his, stepping forward, voice going soft. "Will you marry, Katie?"

She was still confused. "I am. I did."

"I know." He smiled. "But I don't think we got it quite right the first time." Then he nodded to the old chapel. "It's traditional for Harper brides to be married right here."

Kaitlin understood, and her chest tightened with emotion. "You want to..."

"Absolutely. Marry me, Kaitlin. Do it here. Do it now. Love me when you say the vows, and promise my family you'll stay with me forever."

She blinked back the sting of tears. "Oh, Zach."

The ancient door swung open with a groan, and a preacher appeared in the doorway.

"This way," he told them softly, turning, robes rustling as he made his way to the front of the ancient church.

Zach squeezed her hand as they mounted the steps, leading her over the uneven stone floor, past worn wooden pews, to the altar that Lyndall had built for his own wedding, the very first wedding on the island.

Kaitlin swayed sideways against Zach, absorbing the feel of his strong body.

Footsteps sounded behind them, and she glanced back to see Lindsay and Dylan, still dressed for their own wedding.

"Oh, no," she moaned under her breath.

"They insisted," Zach whispered, tucking her arm into the crook of his.

As they stopped at the front of the church, one of the staff members stepped out and handed Kaitlin a bouquet.

White roses.

From Sadie's garden.

It was beyond perfect, and Kaitlin had to blink against the sting of tears.

Lindsay and Dylan took their places, and Zach wrapped an arm around Kaitlin, gathering her close for a private word. "I love you very much, Katie," he whispered.

"And I love you," she whispered back, feeling as though her heart might burst wide open.

His tone went husky as he tenderly stroked her cheek, wiping her tears with the pad of his thumb. "Then, let's take our vows and put this ring on your finger."

* * * * *

COMING NEXT MONTH

Available February 8, 2011

REQUEST YOUR FREE BOOKS!

2 FREE NOVELS PLUS 2 FREE GIFTS!

Passionate, Powerful, Provocative!

YES! Please send me 2 FREE Silhouette Desire® novels and my 2 FREE gifts (gifts are worth about $10). After receiving them, if I don't wish to receive any more books, I can return the shipping statement marked "cancel." If I don't cancel, I will receive 6 brand-new novels every month and be billed just $4.05 per book in the U.S. or $4.74 per book in Canada. That's a saving of at least 15% off the cover price! It's quite a bargain! Shipping and handling is just 50¢ per book.* I understand that accepting the 2 free books and gifts places me under no obligation to buy anything. I can always return a shipment and cancel at any time. Even if I never buy another book, the two free books and gifts are mine to keep forever.

225/326 SDN E5QG

Name	(PLEASE PRINT)

	Apt. #
Address	

City	State/Prov.	Zip/Postal Code

Signature (if under 18, a parent or guardian must sign)

Mail to the **Silhouette Reader Service:**
IN U.S.A.: P.O. Box 1867, Buffalo, NY 14240-1867
IN CANADA: P.O. Box 609, Fort Erie, Ontario L2A 5X3

Not valid for current subscribers to Silhouette Desire books.

Want to try two free books from another line?
Call 1-800-873-8635 or visit www.morefreebooks.com.

* Terms and prices subject to change without notice. Prices do not include applicable taxes. N.Y. residents add applicable sales tax. Canadian residents will be charged applicable provincial taxes and GST. Offer not valid in Quebec. This offer is limited to one order per household. All orders subject to approval. Credit or debit balances in a customer's account(s) may be offset by any other outstanding balance owed by or to the customer. Please allow 4 to 6 weeks for delivery. Offer available while quantities last.

Your Privacy: Silhouette Books is committed to protecting your privacy. Our Privacy Policy is available online at www.eHarlequin.com or upon request from the Reader Service. From time to time we make our lists of customers available to reputable third parties who may have a product or service of interest to you. If you would prefer we not share your name and address, please check here. ☐

Help us get it right—We strive for accurate, respectful and relevant communications. To clarify or modify your communication preferences, visit us at www.ReaderService.com/consumerchoice.

SDES10R

HARLEQUIN®

A Romance

FOR EVERY MOOD™

Spotlight on

Classic

Quintessential, modern love stories
that are romance at its finest.

See the next page
to enjoy a sneak peek from
the Harlequin® Romance series.

*Harlequin Romance author Donna Alward is loved
for her gorgeous rancher heroes.*

*Meet Wyatt as he's confronted by both a precious
little pink bundle left on his doorstep and his neighbor Elli
who's going to show him the ropes....*

Introducing
PROUD RANCHER, PRECIOUS BUNDLE

THE SQUAWKING QUIETED as Elli picked the baby up, and
Wyatt turned around, trying hard to ignore the feelings of
inadequacy as Darcy immediately stopped fussing.

"Maybe she's uncomfortable. What do you think, sweet-
heart?" Elli turned her conversation to the baby.

"What do you think is wrong?" Wyatt asked, putting the
coffee pot back on the burner.

A strange look passed over Elli's face, one that looked
like guilt and panic. But it was gone quickly. "I couldn't
say," she replied.

"But you were so good with her this afternoon." Wyatt
put his hands on his hips.

"Lucky, that's all. I just…remembered a few things."
The same strange look flitted over her features once more.

Wyatt took the coffee to the table. "You fooled me. You
looked like you knew exactly what you were doing." So
much so that Wyatt had felt completely inept. A feeling he
despised. He was used to being the one in control.

Elli and Darcy walked the length of the kitchen and
back. After a few moments, she admitted, "I haven't really
cared for a baby before. The things I thought of were simply
things I'd heard about. Not from experience, Mr. Black."

Her chin jutted up, closing the subject but making him

want to ask the questions now pulsing through his mind. But then he remembered the old saying—*Don't look a gift horse in the mouth.* He'd benefit from whatever insight she had and be glad of it.

"I don't really know what babies need," he said. "I fed her, patted her back like you did, walked her to sleep, but every time I put her down…"

Wyatt almost groaned. Of course. He'd forgotten one important thing. He'd been so focused on getting the formula the right temperature that he'd forgotten to check her diaper. Not that he had any clue what to do there either.

Pulling calves and shoveling out stalls was far less intimidating than one tiny newborn.

"She's probably due for a diaper change, isn't she." He tried to sound nonchalant. This was a perfect opportunity. Elli must know how to change a diaper. He could simply watch her so he'd know better for the next time.

Instead, Elli came around the corner of the counter and placed Darcy back in his arms. "Here you go, Uncle Wyatt," she said lightly. "You get diaper duty. I'll fix the coffee. Cream and sugar?"

Oh boy, Wyatt thought, looking down into Darcy's pursed face, his smug plan blown to smithereens. He was in for it now.

Will sparks fly between Elli and Wyatt?

Find out in
PROUD RANCHER, PRECIOUS BUNDLE
Available February 2011 from Harlequin Romance

Try these Healthy and Delicious Spring Rolls!

INGREDIENTS

2 packages rice-paper
spring roll wrappers
(20 wrappers)

1 cup grated carrot

¼ cup bean sprouts

1 cucumber, julienned

1 red bell pepper, without
stem and seeds, julienned

4 green onions
finely chopped—
use only the green part

DIRECTIONS

1. Soak one rice-paper wrapper
   in a large bowl of hot water
   until softened.

2. Place a pinch each of carrots,
   sprouts, cucumber, bell
   pepper and green onion on the
   wrapper toward the bottom
   third of the rice paper.

3. Fold ends in and roll tightly
   to enclose filling.

4. Repeat with remaining
   wrappers. Chill before
   serving.

Find this and many more delectable recipes
including the perfect dipping sauce in